Brenda Burton—homewrecker?

I never thought I would be "the other woman." I mean, I'm not exactly the femme fatale type. But I'll do whatever it takes to keep Fletch from marrying that awful Dominique. He's so blinded by lust that he can't see her for what she is: a tall, gorgeous…witch.

The fact that *I'm* in love with Fletch is no big secret—well, not to anyone but him. Sally says it's because I'm too nice. The question is: How do I compete with the Girlfriend from Hell? I can't believe I'm actually reading a book called *Land Your Man*. But desperate times call for desperate measures....

Dear Reader,

Land Your Man. That's the name of the book heroine Brenda Burton turns to for help in *A Week 'til the Wedding,* by Beth Henderson. It got me thinking of some of the books friends have given me, all about the rules for meeting and landing (what is he? a fish?) a husband. All I can say is, I hope Brenda's book makes a little more real-world-of-the-nineties sense than the ones I've looked at! And I guess it does, since before too long Fletch Layton is hers for a lifetime. Of course, it probably helps that she's in the market for marriage. Me, I've got better things to worry about.

Like what would I wear if I were going to go to my high school reunion and reencounter the one-time love of my life? That's the least of what's on Kelly Sinclair's mind in Patricia Hagan's *Boy Re-Meets Girl.* She's hoping to find that Robert Brooks has become fat and bald and boring. Too bad for Kelly, he's as irresistible as ever. And this book is pretty irresistible, too.

So have fun with both of this month's selections, and come back next month for two more impossible-to-put-down novels about unexpectedly meeting, dating…and marrying Mr. Right.

Yours truly,

Leslie Wainger

Leslie Wainger
Senior Editor and Editorial Coordinator

Please address questions and book requests to:
Silhouette Reader Service
U.S.: 3010 Walden Ave., P.O. Box 1325, Buffalo, NY 14269
Canadian: P.O. Box 609, Fort Erie, Ont. L2A 5X3

BETH HENDERSON

A Week 'til the Wedding

SILHOUETTE YOURS TRULY™

Published by Silhouette Books
America's Publisher of Contemporary Romance

To all my friends and fellow members of Ohio Valley
Romance Writers of America in Cincinnati.

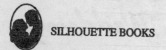 SILHOUETTE BOOKS

ISBN 0-373-52031-X

A WEEK 'TIL THE WEDDING

Copyright © 1996 by Beth Henderson

Printed in U.S.A.

About the Author

Is there a recipe for romance? Well, if you take one song (preferably sung by Sting), add a touch of the Marx Brothers, a heavy dose of finely honed procrastination, and blend them with a self-help book, an ultimatum, elements of your own childhood, a dash of personal work experience and a pinch of lost dreams, you just may get what I got—*A Week 'til the Wedding*.

Not my own, of course. I'm still shopping for Mr. Right. And shopping, and shopping. I love shopping.

The best thing about writing romance, though, is that I get to have affairs with each of my heroes. And there have been a lot of them. *A Week 'til the Wedding* is my third book with Silhouette, but my nineteenth published book.

I'm fickle where romance is concerned, because, once I've typed the final page, it's over between me and the current hero. I'm eager to replace him with another. Eager to dive headlong into love all over again. The only trouble is choosing from among the various heroes lined up in my mind ready to romance me. Sigh! So many men, so little time.

Write me at P.O. Box 262, Englewood, Ohio 45322, and tell me if Fletch was good for you, too.

Love

Beth Henderson

Books by Beth Henderson

Silhouette Yours Truly

A Week 'til the Wedding

Silhouette Special Edition

New Year's Eve #935
Mr. Angel #1002

The Letter

—▸ ◂—

Dearest Fletcher,
The time has come to make up your mind once and for all.

We have been seeing each other exclusively for nearly two years now. I believe that is quite long enough to know what you want.

However, knowing you are a master of procrastination, I am giving you one week—that's seven days, Fletcher—to make a decision. Are you planning to marry me or not?

If the answer is no, I never want to see you again.

If the answer is yes, I will meet you at the trade show in Las Vegas next weekend and we can be married without delay.

I'll be waiting for your answer.

Dominique

1

Day one: Sunday

Fletch Layton groaned and dropped back against his pillow, Dominique's sweetly scented ultimatum clutched between suddenly nerveless fingers. He stared unseeingly at the pattern of swirls on the ceiling while dread crept through his veins. Sunlight spilled in the bedroom window gilding the clothes he'd dropped carelessly on the floor the night before. A robin chirped merrily in an elm in the yard, its mood much better than Fletch's.

But then, Fletch figured, the bird hadn't awakened to find its pleasant bachelor existence threatened.

A deep shudder ran through him at the thought.

Marriage! Now why did Dominique want to go and ruin a perfectly good relationship by evoking the dreaded *M* word? And, perhaps more important, why hadn't he seen it coming?

"You're blind, Layton," he said out loud, his voice grating with self-contempt. "Blind and incredibly stupid."

But then Dominique Morrell was gorgeous enough to make any man blind and stupid. He'd just been more so than the next guy.

She'd tricked him, being so understanding about his bad habits, calling them endearing traits.

He was rarely on time to pick her up. Did she whine?

Nooo.

He always dragged her off to sporting events, even though he knew she detested them. Did she complain?

Nooo. Well, not too loudly.

He'd forgotten her birthday two years running and had procrastinated over shopping for her Christmas present so long that the only outfit he liked had been in an insultingly large size. When she'd opened the gift box and caught sight of the label, her smile had thinned.

But, still, she'd smiled.

Now she was really showing her teeth. And they looked long and glinting from where he lay.

Marriage! Commitment!

Good grief!

The scented piece of paper fluttered from his hand, coming to rest on the opposite side of the bed. The side where he'd expected to find Dominique's warm, curvacious form. The side she expected to occupy for the rest of his natural life. The scent of her musky perfume clung to the bedclothes, reminding him of their enthusiastic coupling the night before.

Fletch groaned again—a bit louder this time—and pushed up out of the bed quickly, anxious to get away from even the faintest reminder of Dominique's presence.

"She's insane, you know," Fletch told his reflection in the bathroom mirror. He ran a hand through his disheveled hair and stared closely at the circles under his eyes. His jawline was a forest of prickly, dark bristles. "She has to be nuts to want to face this mug every morning."

He leaned forward, weight balanced on the heels of his hands against the porcelain sink. "Okay, pal. Fess up. Do you love her? That's what this comes down to, doesn't it?"

No answer sprang readily to his mind. It should, shouldn't it? He'd always thought it should...would.

"You know what your trouble is?" he asked the man in the mirror. "You aren't a morning person. Your brain isn't in gear until high noon."

It still wasn't in gear when the sun crested. A cold shower didn't jump-start it. Neither did a gallon of strong coffee and a belated breakfast of two-day-old cold pizza.

Hoping for a miracle, Fletch stared hard at Dominique's letter. He tried picturing her as he'd first seen her, her mass of coal black curls spilling down her back, her heavenly body displayed in a tiny white bikini as she lounged at poolside. He'd known what he wanted that day, and if anyone had suggested he was putting his neck in a noose in going after it, he would have laughed. What man wouldn't have found a lifetime of making love to that voluptuous body a dream come true? Now it wasn't shapely curves he managed to conjure up, it was a pair of rather flinty-looking dark eyes.

Fletch swallowed loudly.

Outside his window, the robin was joined by some of his buddies, all vocal in their joy over the perfection of the day. The sun smiled down in all its glory. A soft breeze stirred the air, giving pleasant relief from the rising heat. To some, the day would rank as one of the best in creation. But to Fletch, it was beginning to look like the worst day of his life.

Brenda Burton glanced up from her place at her parents' kitchen table when a familiar male voice called a greeting through the back screen door. Without waiting for an invitation, Fletcher Layton pulled it open, strolled into the room and swung Bren's mother into his arms for a familiar hug and kiss.

He'd been making himself at home in the Burton household since he was seven, although there wasn't much of the boy to be seen in his six-foot-two frame now. The tight, faded jeans he wore emphasized the long length of his legs, while the white T-shirt with its bright red-and-blue beer logo emphasized his broad shoulders and lean build. It looked like he hadn't bothered to comb his dark brown hair, which fell forward in thick waves. He hadn't shaved, either, although seeing a bristling masculine face was nothing new in the Burton house. Bren's older brother was razor resistant on weekends, too. But when Fletch pocketed his sunglasses, Bren decided something was up. He looked haggard. It would take more than just a few hours of sleep to erase the circles that hollowed his hazel-green eyes, she decided. Then he flashed his familiar, raffish smile and, as always, Bren felt a bit breathless.

"What a pleasant surprise," Mrs. Burton declared, giving him a fond squeeze in return. "You're just in time to help with the corn."

"What, no steak?" Fletch asked. "I thought that was traditional Sunday fare."

Bren's mother grinned happily at him. "Ground round, and you'll like it, young man," she said with mock severity.

"But first you have to work for it like everyone else," Bren added, tossing him one of the ears of corn she was busy husking.

Fletch caught it one-handed and donned an expression of stunned disbelief. "You'd make a guest work for his supper?"

"Mom makes all moochers work for their supper," Bren said as she stripped dark green leaves from a piece of corn.

"Oh, but don't feel badly, dear," Mrs. Burton soothed softly, patting his bristling cheek. "You're one of my favorite moochers, Fletch. Now sit down and help Bren. She's dawdling over the business so I won't find another job for her. I have to go supervise your father and the charcoal, Bren. The two of you can bring the corn out when it's ready."

As the screen door slammed shut once more, Fletch threw one long leg over the back of a kitchen chair and took his place across from Bren. *"Tsk, tsk,"* he murmured. "Dawdling, are you? I'd never believe it of you, sweetheart."

Bren ripped into a fresh ear. She hated it when he tossed one of his little endearments her way. They'd grown up together. She should be immune to him. But she wasn't. She had gotten the world's worst crush on Fletch when she was thirteen and he was sixteen, and in the ensuing twelve years, she'd never gotten over it.

He didn't know, though.

Frequently, Bren wondered if he even remembered she was from the female branch of the species. To him, she was an old friend, a buddy, a pal. One of the guys.

So she kept her sighs and longings hidden, husbanding them to expend, in an undesignated future, on a man who was less blind to her feminine charms.

The fact that Fletch had helped her land a job in the advertising department of the Bailey and Salazar Corporation, where he was a breath away from a vice presidency, hadn't made it any easier for other Prince Charmings to impress her. It had done just the reverse.

But, since he thought of her as a sort-of-sister, she retaliated by treating him like a brother.

"Can it, Layton," Bren growled, untangling clinging bits of corn silk from her fingers. "What brings you out to the old neighborhood?"

Fletch dealt quickly with an ear, stripping it free of husks. "You do."

Be still my heart, Bren cautioned herself. He didn't mean what she'd like him to mean. If he'd come looking for her there could be only one reason: work.

"I told you to bone up on the latest promotion materials," she said. "But would you listen? Not you.

What's the matter now? Afraid you can't BS your way out of this spot?"

He laughed and tossed the newly cleaned ear of corn aside. "Me? Afraid? Not of a minor little thing like a tube of toothpaste."

Bren picked up his discarded ear of corn and handed it back to him. "Mom likes these closely shaven, slick. You have to pick every bit of silk off it."

"You don't believe me, do you?" Fletch demanded, his tone a bit too overdone to be a reflection of honest emotion. He did begin plucking the finer bits of silk from the corn, though.

Bren concentrated on her own work. "I'll bet you don't even remember what the new toothpaste is called," she said.

Bailey and Salazar was a giant company specializing in soap and personal-care products. Rather than simply slap another New and Improved label on their bestselling fluoride toothpaste, they had decided to launch an entirely new product. Within a few days, Bren and a group of sales personnel would be bound for Las Vegas to push the latest B and S creation at a trade show. As one of the top salespeople, Fletch was to be head honcho on the trip.

Anyone else would have boned up on the promotional matter, but Bren knew Fletch too well to believe that he had. One wit had dubbed him the head BSer at B and S. And, as far as Bren could tell, he was exactly that.

Fletch scowled at her. "I do, too, know what we named the damn toothpaste," he insisted. "It's Virgin Fresh."

"Not," Bren said flatly. She chose another piece of corn and ripped into it. "It's Fresh All Day."

"Can't be. That's a slogan for deodorant."

"Nevertheless . . ."

"You're kidding."

Bren looked at him over the rising pile of empty husks.

"You're not kidding!" Fletch shook his head sadly. "That's the silliest name I ever heard. Why did you let them do it?"

How could she have stopped them? Bren wondered. Fletch might have top management ready to eat out of his hand, but the forces-that-be at Bailey and Salazar weren't about to listen to the opinion of a lowly graphic artist in the ad department.

"So, what do you want to know about the promotion?" Bren asked.

"Hmm. A lot, I suppose. But that can wait. When I called your apartment earlier and didn't get an answer, I guessed there might be a barbecue brewing at the old homestead," he said.

"Just because there has been one every Sunday during the summer for the last twenty years?" Bren asked. "Your thought processes are truly amazing."

Fletch gave her a quelling glance and leaned toward her over the table. "I need you, Brenda," he said quietly.

Bren's mouth went a bit dry. He never called her Brenda. Hardly anybody ever did. He'd also never looked at her with that serious expression and said he needed her before.

"I'm in big trouble," Fletch said.

Bren's bubble burst. What else had she expected?

"I knew you couldn't keep talking your way out of things," she said with a sigh. "It was only a matter of time before the big shots found you out."

Fletch broke the long stalk from a new ear of corn. "Huh? What the hell are you talking about?"

"Your humbug, your con, your—"

"Don't be ridiculous. As far as management is concerned, I've got the golden touch," he said. "The vice presidency is in the bag. I'm not worried about that. It's Dominique that's the problem."

Bren looked at him blankly. "Dominique," she echoed. "The tall, gorgeous bimbo usually draped on your arm?"

"Yeah." Fletch sighed deeply, not bothering to correct the assumption that his girlfriend was a bimbo. "She wants to get married."

"Really? Who to?" Bren asked innocently.

"To me, knucklehead," he said, exasperated.

"Really? Now that's what I call tragic," Bren declared, her voice dripping with sarcasm. "Whatever put that idea into her head, do you suppose?"

"That's what I'd like to know."

"How about the fact that you asked her to move in with you last month?" Bren suggested, leaning back in her seat.

Fletch stripped the ear of corn. "Can't be. She turned me down, remember?"

"Why wouldn't she? You blew it when you pointed out that there was a hookup for her washer and dryer at your place," Bren said.

"I was being considerate about her possessions."

"Not to mention concerned about your pile of dirty laundry," Bren added. She picked up one of the discarded husks and twisted it back and forth between her fingers. "So what's the problem?" she asked. "The woman is drop-dead gorgeous, she owns her own appliances and she wants you. What more could a man ask for in a mate?"

"I wish I knew," Fletch said. "I wish I had an answer."

"Hmm. Very modern of her to ask you to marry her," Bren said. "How did she do it? Down on one knee? Send you flowers? Fix a romantic dinner?"

Fletch finished off the last ear of corn and reached into his back pocket. "She left me this," he said, and casually tossed a crumpled sheet of cream-colored stationery across the table.

Bren let the note lie where it fell. She folded her arms across her chest. "Keep it. I'm not interested in reading your tawdry little love letters."

"Love letter?" Fletch sputtered in indignation. "That scrap of paper is hardly a *love* letter. It's closer to a death threat."

"Yeah?" Intrigued now, Bren carefully picked up the sheet of paper by one corner. "So, what's the big problem?"

"Well, for starters—"

The screen door swung open, then slammed shut with a loud crack. "Hiding out, are you?" Bren's older brother Josh said. He buffeted Fletch from behind, giving him a friendly cuff on the shoulder. "Long time no see."

"Well, I certainly didn't see you anywhere when work had to be done," Fletch declared, punching Josh back in greeting.

Bren got to her feet and began wrapping up the pile of discarded husks. Surreptitiously, she slipped Dominique's letter into the pocket of her jeans. She didn't think Fletch would mind. He wouldn't want Josh to read it, in any case. Of that she was fairly sure.

"Didn't you bring Sally with you today?" she asked.

"Oh, yeah. Sal's talking to Mom and Pop," Josh said offhandedly, far more interested in Fletch at the moment than in his fiancée. "Whaddya say we toss the old baseball around a bit, Fletcher the Catcher?"

Bren expected Fletch to decline. Dominique's interest in marrying him had thrown him for a loop and he needed to talk things through. That's why he'd come seeking her. Bren had been his sounding board for years. Once he worked out his own feelings, she figured, all that would be left for her to do was kiss off her farfetched dreams of Fletch one day falling in love with her.

With this in mind, she was a little surprised to see him get eagerly to his feet, the matter that had brought him to the Burton household apparently forgotten. "Fletcher the Catcher. Dang, I haven't heard that nickname in years," he said. "Baseball equipment still where it was when we were kids?"

"No place else," Josh declared, leading the way out of the room.

Bren watched them leave in stunned silence. Well, what did she expect? If there was one thing that hadn't changed over time, it was Fletch Layton's ability to procrastinate. It was something she'd never understood.

Something she wouldn't do herself.

He'd probably be ready to talk after dinner. If she thought out what to say, what questions to ask him, Fletch would find his way to a decision about his future. All she had to do was be prepared.

And there was only one place to start.

Bren left the corn husks where they were, sank back into her chair and fished out the letter. As she opened it, the cloying scent of Dominique's musky perfume rose from the paper. "Dearest Fletcher," Bren read.

The door had barely swung closed behind Fletch and Josh when Bren heard the squeal of the hinges again and looked up to see her soon-to-be sister-in-law framed in the doorway.

Sally Reiner was petite and fragile looking, from her pale blond hair to her trusting blue eyes. She was dressed casually in walking shorts and a T-shirt, her sun-toned hair spilling around her shoulders. An oversize tote bag was slung over her shoulder.

She looked casually classy, Bren thought, and wondered, not for the first time, what Sally saw in her brother to want to spend her life at his side.

Sally looked back over her shoulder as she slipped into the kitchen. "What's Fletch doing here?" she asked before turning to face Bren. "Or, more importantly, where is Medusa hiding?"

"Dominique isn't here," Bren said as she refolded Fletch's letter and tucked it into the front pocket of her jeans.

"Off terrorizing other hapless victims, is she?" Sally said.

"No doubt," Bren murmured in total agreement. "How have you been holding up since I last saw you? My brother come up with any more really stupid honeymoon suggestions?"

Sally chuckled as she slipped into the chair across from Bren. She dropped her canvas purse on the floor and propped her forearms on the tabletop, leaning forward. "No, I think the fly-fishing idea is still at the head of his list."

"I warned you. It's his ace in the hole," Bren said.

"It didn't work this time," Sally announced, a triumphant gleam in her eye. "Thank goodness I've got the book to fall back on for advice."

"The book?" Bren echoed. "What book?"

Sally's blue eyes widened. "You don't know about *the book?*" She glanced toward the back door, ensuring that they wouldn't be overheard, then reached for the tote bag at her feet and unzipped it. "You have to swear you won't tell Josh or anyone else that I used this."

She handed Bren a hefty tome. The cover was bright, the letters a brilliant red, guaranteed to catch and hold a person's attention.

"It seems only right that I should pass this on to you, now that we're going to be sisters," Sally said.

Bren frowned as she read the volume's title. "*Land Your Man?* You're kidding."

"Hey, it works. All you have to do is follow each step and, *bingo*, you'll be whistling the wedding march," Sally assured her.

"Yeah, right." Bren sneered and handed the book back to her friend.

Sally pushed it away. "I've practically got it memorized, Bren. It's because of the guidance and advice in *Land Your Man* that I'm busy addressing wedding invitations. You could be doing the same."

Fleetingly, Fletch's handsome face flashed in Bren's mind. She pushed the image aside reluctantly and shook her head. "Thanks, Sally, but there's nobody on my line to be reeled in."

"There could be."

"Get real," Bren advised her friend.

"I am!" Sally indicated the book. "This could help."

"Even if self-help books are the trend of the nineties, I'm not that desperate," Bren said.

"You are, too," her future sister-in-law insisted. "You haven't had a date in ages. And I know why."

Bren laughed. "You do?"

"Absolutely. It's because you're too nice."

"Too nice?"

"Think about it," Sally urged. "What woman of our acquaintance has men groveling for her attention?"

"Er..."

"You're being nice again. Be catty. It's Dominique."

Bren thought about Fletch's dilemma with his gorgeous girlfriend. "But she's only interested in one man," she said. "So—"

"There you go again, being naive," Sally said.

"I thought I was nice."

"What's the difference? You and I both know Dominique doesn't care two hoots about him, just what he can give her," Sally declared. "The trouble is, men seem to love bitchy women. God knows why."

"Still—" Bren began.

Sally groaned in disgust. "You're going to defend her, aren't you?"

"Well—"

"Too nice. Too naive," Sally warned. "Don't you think it's time for you to do something nice for yourself?"

"I would, but—"

Sally tapped the self-help book. "Read this," she recommended, "then do something that will make you feel great. Hey! I'll bet taking Fletch away from Dominique would be a real power rush."

"Wha—"

"Stop gasping like a landed fish, Bren. You can do it," Sally insisted. "Fletch would be far happier with you than he is with that Medusa creature."

"But—"

Sally leaned forward over the table. "Personally, he's a little too flaky for my tastes. However, practicing on him would allow you to eliminate some of the steps the book suggests you follow. You already know him fairly well, although I doubt he's worthy of someone of your caliber."

Bren got to her feet. "Wedding planning has obviously weakened your brain or you would never suggest such a thing," she said. "Want some lemonade?"

"Love some. And I am in full possession of all my faculties. This is purely self-defense. I love you dearly, but since Fletch is one of Josh's best friends, if he continues to hang around with Dominique, I'll have to endure her for years to come. You could see this as a crusade. Save Fletch from his own, well, berserk hormones."

Sally paused to catch her breath before asking, "Are you going to take the book?"

Bren sighed deeply as she took glasses from the cupboard and filled them from the pitcher on the counter.

Why her? Perhaps she should have read her horoscope in the paper that morning. Had it carried a warning about friends in need or friends who were well-meaning pests? If only she'd known. She could have pulled the blankets over her head and waited the day out in solitary bliss.

"I am not going to seduce Fletch away from Dominique," Bren insisted. Enticing as the idea was, it was also clearly impossible. He was nuts about the woman. Once he got over his first attack of nerves, he'd be fine and altar-bound.

"Oh, but—" Sally began.

Bren cut her off. "If I do take your silly book, will you stop nagging me?" she demanded, handing her friend the frosty glass of fresh lemonade.

Sally gave her a deceptively innocent grin—the one that disguised Sally's will of iron. "Only if you promise to read it."

Bren gave in. "Oh, all right."

The ball burned into Fletch's glove, making a *plock* sound as it landed. "Not bad, not bad," he called to Josh, all the while hoping his hand would stop stinging. He could still catch—some talents you never lost—but his body was determined to let him know he'd let a few years go by since he'd last tossed a real baseball around. Outside of company-sponsored softball, he'd become a spectator instead of a participant.

Well, there came a time when playing hardball had little to do with baseball. He'd been concentrating on racing up the corporate ladder. When he spun one over home plate now, it was a verbal home run. A ready smile, a steady handshake and the ability to say and do the right thing at the right time had landed him a leap ahead of others. After a brief five years with Bailey and Salazar, he was in line for a comfortable swivel chair in one of the windowed offices reserved for vice presidents.

Fletch tossed the baseball back to Josh, pleased that his throwing arm wasn't as out of shape as his stinging hand seemed to be. He really didn't need this problem with Dominique at this point in his life. Her timing couldn't be worse. He couldn't give the idea of marriage his full attention, not with everything else that was going on—the VP promotion, the toothpaste campaign and...well, things. From his point of view, there were as many pros as there were cons to her proposition. Dominique was gorgeous, which was an asset to a man on his way to the top. And he'd heard the stories about management preferring their team members to be married. It made exec's appear stable, dependable. But Fletch hadn't gotten where he was by doing things the way other people did them. Therefore, marriage was not a key factor where business was concerned.

The ball plunked back into Fletch's glove. He sent it flying back to Josh automatically.

What in the Sam Hill was he supposed to do, anyhow? Give in to Dominique without a fight? Surely there was something in the male code that insisted that he fight tooth and nail before being brought to heel at the altar.

He had no doubt that, sooner or later, that fate would overtake him. It did all men. He just didn't think it was quite his time yet.

Bren would help him; he knew she would. She always did. She'd been his best friend for years. Probably would be for life. Dominique had been jealous at first. There weren't that many guys lucky enough to have a woman as their best friend. But once she met Bren, Dominique had withdrawn her cat's claws quickly. Bren just wasn't the type of female that other females got hypersensitive about.

It wasn't that she was plain. She was really kind of cute, if you liked the pixie-faced, girl-next-door type. He liked her dark curls. They were . . . were . . .

Hmm.

Funny. Instead of the grown-up Bren, he'd just had a flash of the adolescent Bren—all skinny arms and legs and saucer-size eyes, her chin jutting out at a determined angle.

Josh pitched another fast one and Fletch caught it. When he tossed the ball back, he pivoted so that he could glance over at the brick barbecue, where Bren had taken over the burger watch from her dad. The late afternoon sunlight burnished her chestnut curls, playing up the coppery highlights he hadn't realized danced in her hair. The breeze tossed the short locks around her ears and created clusters at her brow and along the long, smooth expanse of her neck. When had she stopped wearing a ponytail? Still, the cap of wild corkscrews suited her. It was rather, um, boyish.

Boyish. Yeah, that was the word he was searching for. It described Bren perfectly.

Of course, she wasn't gangly anymore, but she was definitely tall and slim. He'd always liked long-legged women. Dominique was one, but she was also extremely curvy and very feminine. Bren wasn't. In running shoes, jeans and a comfortable, oversize work shirt, Bren looked generic and sexless. Even at a family cookout, Dominique would have worn sexy shorts and a bandeau top that left lots of skin exposed.

Bren was the kind of girl a guy could be comfortable with. He could be himself. Dominique was a woman who made a man extremely aware of her and of what he'd like to be doing with her.

Still, Fletch had to admit, Bren did have the prettiest green eyes he'd ever seen. They still looked the size of saucers in her small, fey face, but they had alluring depths, like those found in expensively cut gem-stones.

Of course, they'd been narrowed and glaring at him not long ago, but that was just a temporary state of affairs. Bren always came through when he needed her.

And, boy, did he ever need her now!

The baseball went whizzing by his ear.

"Hey! A little less attention on the cook and the food and a little more on the ball," Josh called from across the yard.

"You wouldn't say that if you were close enough to smell those burgers," Fletch yelled backed. "Besides, there is no one more on the ball than I am. Isn't that right, Bren?"

"Is that what you are?" she retorted. "Heaven help us!"

Fletch tossed his glove in the air and caught it again as he strolled over to the barbecue. "She loves me, you know," he told Josh, slipping an arm around Bren's shoulders. "Not a better buddy to be found."

Bren rolled her eyes. "With you as a friend, I'll be a candidate for sainthood, for sure."

Fletch chuckled, then took the long-handled utensil away from her to rescue two of the burgers, as dripping grease made the flames lick higher. "*Tsk, tsk.* Forgotten I like my beef on the rare side, sweetheart?"

"You won't get it done that way in this household," Josh said.

Bren stepped aside. "Then have at it," she offered, a mischievous grin enhancing the pixieish cast of her face.

Well, damn! She was actually pretty! Strange he'd never noticed that before, Fletch mused. He had a reputation as a connoisseur of women. But that was the way it was with people you knew forever. You never really saw them.

Bren moved farther back from the grill. "I'm going to take a real chance here," she said, "and leave the cooking in your amateurish hands." Her grin widened. "Dad said that if I looked incompetent enough I'd find a sucker to take over. Oh, and Mom wants to know what you both want to drink. Lemonade, iced tea..."

"Beer," Fletch and Josh said in unison.

Once she was striding across the yard toward the back door, Josh dropped down in a lounge chair, slumping deep into the cushions, and stretched out his legs. "Amateur! Do you believe that? Hell, when a man can't out-barbecue a woman the world will come to an abrupt end."

Fletch flipped the other burgers over, glancing back at Bren. She had a nice womanly twitch to her walk. Funny he'd never noticed that before, either. It was rather enticing the way the long tail of her shirt swayed with each step. "Maybe so, but Bren's not like other girls," he said.

"Don't let her hear you call her a girl," Josh cautioned. "They don't like that these days. They are women, as if that was a completely different breed of being."

"Well, it is," Fletch said. A pillar of smoke rose from the barbecue and drifted toward him on the breeze, bringing with it the distinct scents of burning charcoal and cooking meat. "Let's face it, pal. They are different. Girls you can understand. Women you never will. But there are exceptions to the rule. Like Bren."

Josh's grunt was definitely one of disagreement.

"No, no. Think about it," Fletch urged. "For instance, did we ever have any trouble getting your sister to do things our way?"

Josh's brow clouded. "What do you mean?"

"We told her to eat a worm and she did it, didn't she?"

"She was seven and a pest, always tagging along after us."

"I didn't mind as much as you did," Fletch said. A larger cloud of smoke rose from the white coals. "Remember that summer when our team was going into the championships and the shortstop broke his leg?"

"Yeeeah . . ." Josh said carefully. "I think so."

"Who talked us into the sweetest deal ever made?"

Josh shrugged. "Search me. Who?"

"Bren."

"And?" Bren's brother prompted.

Fletch turned away from the sizzling burgers. "You don't remember? Hell, she was the best damn shortstop we ever had. We snapped up the championship that year because of her."

"We did? I thought it was my home run in the final inning."

"Dreamer. You never had a home run in your life," Fletch insisted. The cloud of smoke was denser now. It engulfed him as flames licked hungrily at the cooking burgers. "Now I, on the other hand," he continued, waving the smoke away, "was headed for the baseball hall of—"

Josh leapt to his feet and snatched the barbecue utensil from Fletch's hand. "You are a disgrace to the male barbecuing race."

Fletch grinned at Josh and flopped back into his friend's recently deserted lawn chair. "You'll notice I'm not the sap doing the cooking now. And you thought I was stupid."

"Well, you are," Josh said. "You're waxing poetic over Bren."

"I was reminiscing."

"Didn't sound like it to me." Josh rearranged the food, getting the meat away from the grease-fueled flames. "You always did have something going with Bren, though," he mused.

Fletch sat up straighter. "With Bren? Come on. She's a pal, but—"

"Come off it," Josh growled. "I don't mean you've got the hots for her. Not when dishes like Dominique are all over you." He sighed wistfully. "Still, Bren was game for anything, wasn't she? Even taking that daredevil jump on her bike over Hobson's Creek."

She'd broken her arm doing it and had gotten a nasty gash in her forehead, Fletch recalled. He wondered if she still had the battle scar from that day. How old had they all been? "I told her it couldn't be done," he murmured.

"Which, as you and I both know, is why she tried it. I might have been her brother, but you were the one she looked up to," Josh said. "I think these things are charred enough to be called real home cooking. At least, Burton family home cooking."

Fletch grinned. "That's why I came."

Josh snorted. "The hell it is. You came to see Bren. And why you should is beyond me."

Bren watched the sky change from a pearl gray to a darker Harris-tweed gray spotted with sex-crazed fireflies. The erratic flash of the bugs' taillights turned the yard into a miniature solar system. Was it the males or the females that were into Morse code? she wondered. She'd learned which in a science class once, but the information was gone. Only the part about the flashing lights being a mating dance remained.

And that had only surfaced because she'd been too close to Fletch all afternoon. Her brain was mushy with the effort of having to be a buddy when she secretly dreamed, hopelessly, of being more.

"I wonder what it would be like to be a bug?" she mused out loud as the screen door swung open.

"Not good," Fletch said, dropping down beside her on the porch swing. He stretched out his long legs, resting his heels on the porch railing. His running shoes looked like they had run their course, but they'd been his favorites since he'd been in college, she knew. She wondered if he ever wore them around Dominique. Probably not. He was only comfortable enough to be a slob around Bren.

Lucky me, she thought.

"Bugs have got a short life span," Fletch said. "What with people hating their guts and hiring pesticidal hit men to wipe out their families, it is not an easy existence."

Bren gave the swing a push, setting it to swaying gently. It wasn't enough to knock Fletch's feet off the railing. She considered pushing harder.

"Given this a lot of thought, have you?" she asked.

"Not a bit, actually." He grinned over at her. It was his lazy smile, the one that tightened her stomach in mating-dance knots.

"Your team losing?" she asked, forcing her voice to sound calm and in control. After dinner the men had disappeared into the family room, and a battle for possession of the remote control had ensued. One sports show after another had flicked by in rapid succession since then. While her mother and Sally put their heads together over the upcoming wedding, Bren had slipped out of the kitchen to join the men before the TV, but when the home team's game ended, she'd drifted out again.

"Naw, my team's ahead," Fletch said. "But it's a rather boring game. Nothing's happened in four innings."

"That mean you're finally ready to talk?"

He looked a bit guilty. He should, she thought. He'd been in such a rush to get her advice, but since he'd asked for it, sidestepping was all Fletch had been doing.

"Actually, I'm ready to leave," he said. "I've got a spot waiting for me in the boardroom at tomorrow's meeting."

Bren took Dominique's note from her pocket and passed it back to him. She'd finally managed to read it, but other than thinking Dominique could have been a bit more diplomatic in her phrasing, had not given it much thought herself. Sally's book was an entirely different matter. Bren hadn't been able to get it off her mind.

"So, what have you decided to do about the letter?" she asked.

Fletch shoved the already crumpled note in his jeans pocket. "Nothing. At least for now." His grin widened. "Hey, what's the hurry with Dominique, anyway? I've still got six days to answer her ultimatum."

"Fletch..."

He flicked a finger along Bren's cheek in a casual caress. "Don't sweat it, sweetheart. We'll talk tomorrow. How about lunch?"

She frowned. "I don't know. There's still a lot to be done if we're leaving on Tuesday for the trade show in Vegas."

"Tell you what. I will personally volunteer to help with anything that isn't tied up tomorrow. But only after lunch."

"Well..." Bren knew better, but she wavered. She always did when he was in his coaxing mode. She always had. She had the scars to prove it, too.

Fletch got to his feet. "Great. It's a date. Think about where you want to go. I've got an expense account that's just itching to be used."

"Fletch—"

"In fact," he said, "we'll make sure it's a legit expense, something to do with the toothpaste promotion. I'll say Virgin Fresh and—"

"And I'll correct you, as usual. It's Fresh All Day."

"Damn. Well, I'll get it yet," he promised breezily and swung a leg over the porch rail. "Adios. And thanks for being such a great friend, Bren. Don't know what I'd do without you."

Bren watched him stride across the lawn, carving a path through the overexcited lightning bugs. He slid into his car, blinked the headlights twice in farewell and backed out into the street.

If he was emulating the courting fireflies, Bren thought, he was doing a lousy job.

But if that was true, why did she always feel so desolate each time he left her?

Would she ever learn?

2

Day two: Monday
  Love is a lot like war. This book is your hand-
  book of winning strategy. Start by throwing him
  off-balance. Do something unexpected.
                                    Land Your Man

Calling the antibacteria toothpaste *Virgin* had been
a joke that began when the product was little more
than a vague idea thrown out during an informal
meeting of staffers in the product-development department. The meeting had been held during happy
hour at an establishment a block from the main Bailey and Salazar office complex. During the months it
took for the idea to become reality, word of the
toothpaste's nickname spread through the company as
swiftly as the flu virus did when holiday weekends approached. What else could it be called when the stuff
claimed to keep a person's mouth free of germs all
day? It was better than mouthwash, better than breath
mints, better than chewing gum. It was so good—or
so someone in the sales department had been heard to

claim—that the division of B and S that made tooth-brushes was expecting a drop in revenue, since frequent brushing would be nearly a thing of the past.

While enthusiastic about the new toothpaste, top management felt the name needed a lot more work than the product and turned the matter over to the advertising department. Bren's department. As a result, "Virgin" had been quickly rebaptized "Fresh All Day."

The trouble was, everyone had referred to it as Virgin for so long that the nickname had become a habit.

When Bren pulled into the Bailey and Salazar parking lot a few minutes before eight, her mind was on the project. For months she had slaved over the Fresh All Day promotion. It hadn't been just a change of name they'd sweated out, it had been the tube packaging, the choice of models, the choice of typeface, the catchy jingle and the timing of television and magazine ad blitzes. As a graphic artist, she worked closely with copywriters, photographers, video producers, printers, demographic and geographic marketing experts and her harried boss—a man who had just as much trouble remembering the product's official name as Fletch did.

It was partly due to rampant memory failure, particularly in the departments connected with the new product, that a large billboard now stood at one side of the company parking lot. Eight-foot-tall letters announced Fresh All Day, while a giant tube of toothpaste—"the tube that ate Cleveland," Bren's boss had been heard to quip—cast a hulking shadow over employees as they entered or left the area. The message was clear: remember the official name or else.

Thus, Bren was not alone when she exited the elevator mumbling "Fresh All Day" under her breath. Nearly everyone was.

She spent a good part of the morning tracking down the whereabouts of the newest ad-campaign poster and double-checking plane and hotel reservations. The rest of the advertising-department staff were equally frantic, each member fretting over a different list of priorities. Until Fresh All Day was launched, Bailey and Salazar's other products were conveniently forgotten.

The department as a whole had collapsed at their desks for a well-deserved coffee break when Fletch poked his head in the open door. He flashed a grin the equal of those on the Fresh All Day commercials. "Everything ready to go for Virgin Fresh?" he asked.

A hail of paper wads assaulted him from around the room.

"What did I say?" he demanded. He ambled over to perch on a corner of Bren's desk.

This was a completely different Fletch from the one she'd seen the day before. His hair was styled back from his face and brushed to a high mahogany sheen. His jaw was freshly shaved, allowing the faint cleft in his chin to reappear. His slate gray three-piece suit, white shirt and subdued striped tie were impeccable. If she looked down, Bren was nearly sure she'd see her own face reflected in the bright polish of his black loafers.

Rather than look, though, Bren leaned back in her chair and tossed him a small sample package of toothpaste. "What's that say?" she asked.

He glanced down at the bright turquoise lettering on the oatmeal-colored box. "Oops."

"I've heard rumors that the brass is considering installing a nice medieval rack to use on anyone who can't remember the new name," she said.

"Then I hope you like me as much when I'm taller as you do now," Fletch said, patently unconcerned. "Did you come up with an idea of where you want to have lunch?"

"All I've thought about today is our trip tomorrow. There's still so much to be done I'm not sure I can even get away for lunch." Elbows on the arms of her chair, Bren held her coffee mug between her hands and sipped. She was going to need all the caffeine she could get if she intended to make it through the day.

Fletch took the mug away from her and gulped a swallow himself. "You have to take a lunch break. We have that problem to discuss."

"You could solve it without me," she suggested.

He looked skeptical.

"Yes, yes," Bren purred. "I know it's a radical idea, but you could do it if you wanted to."

"No, I couldn't," Fletch insisted. "I've tried to sleep on the idea, figuring that I'd wake up with an answer clear in my mind, but it didn't work. I had nightmares all night."

"Dominique chasing you with a pickax?"

"Worse." Fletch shivered dramatically. "There were tubes of toothpaste with bright white, piano-keyboard smiles everywhere I turned."

"Chasing you, were they?"

"Dancing the rumba, actually, complete with Carmen Miranda headdresses instead of screw-on caps."

"Interesting."

"Yeah, I thought you'd like the concept."

"Sounds like deep down you're afraid you're going to foul up on the Fresh All Day promotion," Bren said.

Fletch smirked. "What is this? Psych 101?"

"Hey, I'm not the one who's dreaming about toothpaste," Bren insisted.

"You're also not the one who ate a third chili dog at ten o'clock last night. I should have turned it down when your mom offered it," Fletch said. "Are after-dinner snacks always that lethal at your parents' house?"

"Only when Josh is visiting. Mom thinks he's wasting away."

"Yeah, right. He did look a little peaked. All two-hundred-plus pounds of him," Fletch said. He buried his nose in Bren's mug of coffee once more.

Bren sighed. "You don't need me to make a decision about..." She glanced to where a couple of her associates stood waiting for a fresh pot of coffee to brew. It wouldn't do to broadcast news of Dominique's ultimatum to the rumormongers. She lowered her voice. "About, well, you know."

"Don't make it sound like I've got an infectious disease," Fletch declared. "I just need a friend's advice, that's all."

"So I'm supposed to hold your hand while you blither your way into a decision?"

Fletch finished off her coffee. "Something like that."

Bren closed her eyes and groaned. "Wouldn't it be better to have Dominique hold your hand? Talk to her about your feelings. Tell her—"

The telephone on the desk buzzed. "Is Mr. Layton there?" the sales secretary asked when Bren answered. "I'm trying to locate him. There is an emergency meeting in the boardroom."

"I'll tell him," Bren promised and dropped the receiver back in the cradle. "Destiny is calling you," she told Fletch. "Boardroom, now. My guess is they've got the rack installed."

He rose to his feet, checked the set of his tie and shot his cuffs. "I'll try to be brave. I'll also be back at one to take you to lunch."

"Fletch—"

He gave her a slow smile. "At one, Bren. Don't stand me up."

As if she ever would, Bren thought as she watched him slip out the door. As if she ever could.

As ordered, Bren was ready to leave when Fletch reappeared a few hours later. "No more than thirty minutes," she insisted. "That's all I can spare."

"Don't be ridiculous," he told her. "We're discussing business, remember?" He stuck his head in her boss's office. "I'm taking Bren to lunch so she can fill me in on all the last-minute changes for the Vegas trip. I've got no idea when we'll be back," he said. "Any objection?"

Before there could be one, Fletch left the office, firmly pushing Bren ahead of him.

"So what are we having?" he asked. "French gourmet, surf and turf, Chinese, Italian?"

"I'm only taking half an hour," Bren informed him, the tone of her voice indicating she would be inflexible over changes he might try to make on the time limit. She leaned on the elevator call button. "That means we walk across to the park and hit the vendor wagons."

Fletch grimaced. "I don't think I can handle another hot dog this soon."

"I was thinking more of a hot pretzel."

"That's it?"

"And a large iced tea."

"You'll waste away to nothing," Fletch said.

The elevator arrived and people returning from their own hastily gulped lunches spilled out. Bren squeezed between them and into the elevator before the doors snapped closed again. Fletch was a step behind her. When she hit the button for the first floor, he realized they had the lift all to themselves—yet he continued to stand close to her.

He was more aware of her than he'd ever been before.

Hmm...now this is interesting, he mused, but made no effort to move away. The overhead lighting picked up the same coppery lights he'd noticed in her hair the day before.

"When did you start wearing your hair that way?" he asked.

Bren gave him a disgusted look. "Two years ago."

"Oh. Did I tell you then that it looks nice?"

"No."

"Well, it does," Fletch said.

"Thank you," Bren answered.

They fell silent. The elevator hummed, working its way down the high rise at an unhurried pace.

"That's a nice perfume," he commented after a while.

"I'm not wearing perfume. It's soap."

"Scented though."

"Bailey and Salazar's best," she said.

The elevator dropped another floor.

"Lavender, huh?" Fletch said.

"Lilac. You never could tell one flower from another."

"True," he admitted.

The lift reached the ground floor. The doors opened smoothly to display a horde of anxious workers waiting to board. His hand placed intimately along Bren's spine, Fletch pushed their way through. She moved away from his touch the moment there was enough space to do so.

"You sure all you want is a pretzel?" he demanded as they stepped out of the lobby into bright sunlight. "It's hot as blazes out here."

"So take your suit coat off," she suggested, and strode across the street. "You're a real wimp anymore."

Fletch tugged at his tie, loosening the knot at his throat. "Am not," he insisted, shedding adulthood as quickly as he did his jacket.

Bren turned to face him, skipping backward as she walked. "Are, too," she said, grinning widely.

Fletch unbuttoned his vest. "So where's the pretzel vendor?"

"Near the fountain."

"There's a fountain in this park? Can't be. It's only a city block wide," he said, incredulity filling his voice.

"You big executives," Bren moaned sadly, shaking her head. Her curls danced.

Fletch had a sudden urge to bury his fingers in her dark tresses and breathe deeply of her lilac-scented, soap-scrubbed skin. The impulse floored him, causing him to come to a complete standstill. What was the matter with him? This was Bren. His buddy.

"So, which way?" he asked, looking around. Anything so that she wouldn't spot the hint of man-woman awareness in his eyes.

"Follow me," Bren instructed.

He was more than willing to do so. It let him examine the feminine sway of her walk, the one he'd only noticed the day before.

Today she was wearing a cream-colored linen pantsuit. The jacket was long, but still shorter than her shirttail had been on Sunday. It wasn't as flirty in action.

"There it is," Bren announced, pointing to a cart with a brightly colored canvas awning.

It was parked in the shade near a tinkling fountain that featured a small, moss-tinted statue. The classically gowned woman held a jar, from which flowed a lazy trickle of water.

Fletch had to admit the setting looked cool and inviting.

But then, so did Bren when she smiled at him.

Get a grip on yourself, Layton, Fletch ordered silently. This was Bren, his childhood friend. She was not the woman of his dreams; Dominique was that. Or should be. At any rate, his new awareness of Bren was disturbing, and it wasn't helping him concentrate on more-pressing matters.

It was probably just the heat that was making him crazy. He'd been out in the sun tossing a ball around yesterday when the first symptoms of this particular disease had struck, and here he was standing in the middle of a sun-drenched park being boiled alive again. It had to be the humidity or sunstroke. Under normal circumstances he would not find himself attracted to Bren.

An elderly man was seated close by the vendor wagon, a Reds baseball cap pulled low over his eyes. When he saw Bren and Fletch, he pushed himself slowly to his feet. Fletch could hear the plastic webbing of the man's lawn chair creak with the movement.

"Hi, Henry," Bren said in greeting. "I'll have a pretzel with—"

Fletch cut her off. "With mustard. Just a squiggle of it," he told the vendor before turning to face her. "See, I remember."

Bren wasn't impressed with this dazzling display. "Oh, Henry knows how I like it," she assured Fletch breezily before turning back to the elderly man. "With a tall iced tea today, Henry. Three sugars. What'll you have, Fletch?"

My head examined, he thought. "Another of the same," he said. "And if I need my stomach pumped later today, Bren, just make sure you tell the hospital staff that this was your idea."

"Oh, you'll survive," she said as she thanked Henry for her strange meal and moved off to a park bench while Fletch paid for everything.

She'd chosen a bench in the shade of a tall maple tree, unconcerned that it appeared to have served as a target in the past by birds. Fletch eyed it suspiciously before tossing his discarded jacket over the back and taking a seat next to her.

Bren barely let him settle before launching an attack. Or at least, it seemed like one to Fletch. "Why don't you want to get married?" she demanded.

He took a hasty bite of his mustard-smeared lunch to stall for time. "I didn't say I didn't," he mumbled.

Bren pondered his response a moment. "Then you're merely unsure about marrying Dominique?"

"Yes. No." He watched the way dappled sunlight played over Bren's hair and shoulders. She wore a silky-looking turquoise blouse with a scooped neck beneath her jacket, and a primitive bleached-stone-and-natural-twine necklace dangled over her breast. "You look really nice today," he said. "Did I mention that?"

"Don't change the subject," Bren recommended. "The clock is ticking. How do you feel about Dominique?"

"At the moment? Far from kind."

"And before you got her letter?"

Fletch gulped at his tea. "Er, that's not exactly the kind of thing you tell another girl."

"Don't think of me as another girl," Bren said. "You never did before, so why start now?"

Good question. If only he had an answer!

"I'll just take it that you were feeling very fond of Dominique prior to her proposal," Bren continued. "Which seems to mean that you would not be averse to spending more time with her."

"More time, as in a lifetime?"

"Exactly," Bren said. "So, what do you think?"

"It's not that easy. In fact, it's... You know, you should have saved that outfit for the trade show," Fletch said. "It's the same colors used on the Virgin Fresh box."

"That's not the name...oh, forget it. You're hopeless," Bren declared. She concentrated on her soft pretzel.

"Well, I mean it," Fletch insisted. "You really do look nice today."

"Hmmph," Bren mumbled.

He figured she'd thanked him. "I was just trying to remember if I've ever seen you in anything other than slacks, though. Do you own any skirts? Dresses?"

Bren frowned. "Of course I do," she said—lying, he was sure—before turning doggedly back to the subject at hand. "Now, I think that you're only having trouble knowing what you want because ... What are you looking at?"

He bent a bit, squinting his eyes for a clearer look as he peered at her face. "You still have a scar," he said.

Bren's hand went self-consciously to the tiny white arc on her temple.

"I wondered if you did." Fletch leaned back against his suit jacket, pleased with his discovery. "We had some great times together when we were kids, didn't we?"

Bren looked at him.

She'd give an alien from outer space that same suspicious consideration, Fletch decided.

"Speak for yourself, bub," Bren said. "You and Josh specialized in putting me through hell more often than not."

"We did?" Fletch chewed thoughtfully on a bite of pretzel. "You're thinking about the senior prom, aren't you?"

"That's one example," Bren allowed.

"We were just protecting you," Fletch explained. "We knew what guys were like, what they were after. You were a complete innocent and—"

"And you both made sure I stayed that way, whether I wanted to or not," Bren finished. "I was so embarrassed. I could have cheerfully killed you."

"You deserved better than a no-neck linebacker with an IQ of sixty," Fletch said.

"I was lucky he had the guts to ask me out. There weren't many guys who did, considering I had you and Josh daring them to cross some invisible line. But when you shadowed our every move..." Bren growled with the memory of ancient—not to mention pent-up—frustration.

Fletch looked unrepentant. "Well, you still forgave us, didn't you?"

"Who says I did?" Bren snapped. "It was the worst night of my life." She tore into the last of her soft pretzel, teeth bared as she relived prom night. "At least things got better when I went away to college and escaped you guys."

Escaped? Had he and Josh been that bad? For that matter, what was wrong with being protective of her? They hadn't wanted her to be hurt. Hadn't wanted some oversexed dolt using her in the heat of the moment, then dumping her. Hadn't wanted her to experience what they'd done to other girls without a thought.

And now here he was, starting to have those same base thoughts about her himself.

Fletch downed the last of his tea and found Bren consulting her watch.

"Well, I don't suppose I should be surprised that we got nowhere with your problem," she said. "But my time is up. You'll have to grapple with it yourself."

Which problem did she mean? The one where he found himself drawn to her or the one where he had to give an answer to Dominique? Somehow, that last one was losing its immediacy for him.

"You've only got five days left before you have to tell Dominique what's what," Bren reminded him.

The proverbial time clock was ticking louder, rather like a bomb in a television crime show.

Fletch made a snap decision. "Well, you know very well that I'll keep putting things off if you don't goad me into action," he said.

"So I'm to wield the cattle prod?" Bren asked. She dusted her hands with a napkin, then patted it to her mouth to remove any traces of mustard that remained.

"I'm a master procrastinator, Bren. You've got to help me."

She met him eye-to-eye. Fletch fought down a new rush of unwelcome awareness. She did have the most gorgeous green eyes, though.

Bren sighed. "Okay. I'll stick by you a while longer. But not right now. It's a madhouse in advertising. We can talk about all of this tomorrow on the plane to Vegas."

"Too late," Fletch said. "Let's make it dinner tonight. A nice, long, sit-down dinner."

"Fletch!" she wailed. "Don't you understand? I'm working late and—"

"Make it eight. I'll pick you up at your apartment. Oh, and can you wear a dress? I'll take you someplace better than a city park."

"I—"

He glanced down, studying the cream-colored flats she wore. "High heels? You own a pair?" he asked.

"What's got into you?"

"Panic, sweetheart," Fletch declared with heart-felt emotion. "Pure, unadulterated panic." He wasn't about to tell her what he was really worried about, though. Instead, he promised himself, he was going to test these new shoal-filled waters. And he was going to begin that very night. At dinner.

Moments later Bren slumped at her desk and tried to fathom what was up with Fletch. She was overly familiar with his ability to put things off until the last minute. Actually, the more important the decision, the more he was inclined to drag his feet.

She'd had a ringside seat for a good number of his procrastiganzas already. There had been his frequent late arrivals at high school and at numerous sporting events. His hastily mailed applications for college. His pleading at various professors' offices for admittance to closed classes and at her door to have papers typed hours before they were due. He hadn't prepared for a single exam earlier than dawn of the day of the test, a talent he continued to use in preparing for B and S sales meetings. The pièce de résistance, however, was his yearly panic with income-tax forms, complete with late-night drives to the post office for the official last-minute postmark.

Procrastination was a science to Fletch, so Bren wasn't surprised that he was unwilling to discuss committing himself to marriage without first enjoying a spell of waffling over the decision. In fact, Bren was pretty sure that until Dominique had delivered her ultimatum, Fletch hadn't given marriage a moment's thought. When he'd asked Dominique to move in with him, the only long-term commitment he'd considered had been to his own comfort. And to his laundry.

So what was he up to now? Although Bren considered herself fairly good at following the rambling thought processes of her longtime friend, he had thrown her this time. What was he doing, complimenting her on her hair? On her outfit? Why had he asked her to wear a dress and high heels tonight? They'd shared dinner often enough over the years, but it had always been a sandwich at a sports bar. There was no way she was dressing up to perch on a bar stool and guzzle beer while he found new ways to avoid committing himself to Dominique until the very last minute.

Which he would do. If he had until 6:00 a.m. Sunday, he'd probably call at 5:59 a.m. to propose.

Bren sighed deeply and tried to turn her attention back to the task at hand. As part of the Las Vegas–bound team of B and S associates, she had the job of making sure everything ran smoothly at the trade show. She hadn't been kidding when she told Fletch she was pressed for time. There were at least *two* lists of things she hadn't even glanced at yet, much less done, and—

A cloud of musk-scented perfume surrounded Bren a moment before she heard the purr of a throaty female voice behind her. "Brenda, dear. Might I have a word with you?"

Bren clenched her teeth. Wasn't it bad enough that Fletch pestered her with his problems? Now his lady love, from B and S's consumer relations division, had come to bother her, too.

Bren wasn't sure if she could handle hearing Dominique gush about her feelings for Fletch. What would they be—tales of undying love? A tearfully confessed desire to have his children? To cook his dinner? Wash his socks?

Bren forced her lips into the semblance of a smile before turning to greet Fletch's future bride. "Dominique. Long time no see. To what do I owe this—" Bren forced the final word out "—pleasure?"

Her movements catlike, Dominique flowed onto the corner of Bren's desk, the same spot where Fletch had perched earlier. Her legs crossed with an exotic whisper of silk. The slim, short skirt of her fire-engine red dress rose to give the men around the room a wider expanse of thigh to ogle. She moved her head, tossing long, spiraling black curls over her shoulder, and composed her features into a pout.

"Well," she began with a breathy little sigh, "I have a teensy confession to make. I need your help."

Mentally, Bren groaned.

"Woman-to-woman, I would appreciate your assistance," Dominique said.

Yeah, right.

"No one knows Fletcher as well as you do, Brenda dear. And, considering the two of you had lunch together, I'm sure that you know about my suggestion."

Suggestion, huh? Fletch had termed Dominique's little love note an ultimatum, a death threat. It was amazing, Bren thought, how neither of them ever called the letter what she saw it as—a marriage proposal. Was she the only one with a romantic soul?

"Considering Fletcher uses you as his sounding board, I'm sure you will be the first to note a trend to his thoughts," Dominique continued. "And I'm sure you understand how much I'd appreciate any help you can lend to guide those thoughts in an appropriate direction."

In a pig's eye, Bren thought. If Fletch was going to marry the witch, he was going to have to make the decision on his own—cut his own throat, so to speak.

Bren forced her expression to be neutral and leaned back in her desk chair, pretending to be relaxed. Pretending that her back didn't arch like a cat's whenever Dominique came within spitting distance. "I'm afraid I have no idea what you are talking about, Dominique."

The other woman frowned slightly, two small grooves appearing over the bridge of her nose. They reminded Bren of tiny horns.

"I was sure that Fletcher took you to lunch to discuss the decision he has to make," Dominique said. "What else could it have been?"

"Business?" Bren suggested, figuring Fletch's girlfriend wouldn't catch on to how improbable that idea was. "We do leave for the trade show tomorrow, and as head of this sales foray, he does need to be up-to-date on the product promotional plans." The small devil perched on her shoulder made Bren add a final tag. "Next to the launch of Fresh All Day, everything else pales."

While Dominique fumed, Bren picked a sheet of paper off her desk and pretended to be totally engrossed in it.

"This is far more important than a new toothpaste," Dominique said.

"Tell that to the stockholders," Bren murmured, her head still bent over her pseudowork.

Dominique plucked the paper from Bren's hand. "The matter I expected Fletcher to have consulted you about is of interest to me," she hissed.

Merely "of interest." Not "of great interest" or "of particular interest."

"I'm sure it is," Bren said smoothly, reclaiming her To Do list from Dominique's fingers. "Could you move? I think you're sitting on page two of this." She rattled the sheet of paper for effect.

Dominique didn't budge. If anything, she seemed to grow roots. "If Fletcher hasn't spoken to you yet, I'm sure he will soon," Dominique insisted, her voice stern, her eyes cold and hard.

That would be just the way she'd look when she told Fletch's children they had misbehaved. Which, being Fletch's kids, they would do frequently, Bren figured, briefly pitying the as-yet-unconceived Layton tykes.

With Dominique's inflexible glare fixed on her, Bren resisted the urge to grind her teeth. Although she hadn't wanted to hear Dominique confess the depth of her love for Fletch, the fact that the woman hadn't mentioned tender feelings of any kind, that she didn't appear to even consider love necessary for marriage, put Bren on the defensive where her childhood friend was concerned.

Unaware that her listener's eyes had narrowed, Dominique considered the long, clawlike, scarlet-painted nails of her right hand. "I've proposed a merger to Fletcher," she said. "And although I've allowed him time to consider it, I really don't feel he need dawdle over the decision. I was hoping that you could..."

"Give him a push?" Bren suggested innocently.

Dominique gave her a slight and very insincere smile. "I was going to say give him guidance, Brenda dear. I know that Fletcher respects your opinions and..."

Bren tuned her out. Dominique had been dating Fletch for two years and she still didn't know a damn thing about him. He respected Bren's opinion? Boy, was that a joke! He might consider someone else's opinion occasionally, but only to use as a means to his own ends. Of course, what could she expect from a woman who, after two years as his nearly constant companion, was still blind to the fact that Fletch detested the name Fletcher?

"I know you'll agree with me that Fletcher's tendency to quibble over decisions is quite irritating," Dominique said.

A nanosecond before, Bren might have, but now she found his procrastination to be an endearing trait. What *was* irritating was Dominique's bloodless attitude.

"I can't say that I've noticed Fletch quibbling over decisions," Bren fibbed with a straight face. "But then I'm not looking at him with the eyes of a woman in love. You are that, right? You do love him?"

The corners of Dominique's scarlet-lipstick-coated mouth curved slightly. "What a ridiculous question. Of course I do. I'm very fond of Fletcher."

Only fond? *What a fool you are, Fletch,* Bren thought. *Two years of your life spent panting at the woman's heels and she's* fond *of you.*

"As I know you'll agree, Brenda dear, Fletcher is clay waiting to be molded."

Dominique had to be kidding. Mold Fletch? Oh, he could annoy the most patient of saints, but that wouldn't necessarily stop even if a woman did manage to change him. Besides, what was there about him that cried to be altered?

Dominique laughed lightly. "The difficulty would be in deciding where to begin. There are so many areas in which he needs improvement."

No longer even making an attempt to act as if she was interested in getting back to work, Bren bared her teeth in a rather feral smile. "Such as?" she prompted, her cheeks burning with spots of anger.

Dominique didn't notice the far-from-friendly smile. "Well, the depressing enthusiasm he has for those distasteful sporting events, for one. Or his tendency to attract the most disreputable friends."

Bren figured she and her brother headed that list— at least in Dominique's little mind.

"And, of course, there is his lack of vision in regard to the future."

Bren nearly gaped. "Lack of vision? He's going to be the youngest vice president the company has ever had!"

"Yes, but why stop there? Why not become president or chairman of the board?" Dominique fairly oozed with personal ambition. "Fletcher needs to turn his talents to politics. That is where real power lies."

"But—but..." Bren sputtered.

"Oh, don't remind me of the way he bleats about hating politics," Dominique recommended with a careless wave of her scarlet-clawed hand. "He's a natural politician. He can talk anyone into doing anything. You, I'm sure, know that, Brenda dear. As I understand it, in convincing you to do a number of disgusting things, Fletcher and your brother made your childhood a sheer hell."

Hell? Well, maybe Bren had thought so herself at times, but compared to the childhood she surmised Dominique had had, it had been paradise. Bren had been treated as an equal by Fletch and Josh, especially after proving herself, and had spent all her time with the two boys she loved most in the world. When they'd all grown up, Josh had drifted away, more interested in himself than in his sister, but Fletch had always been there for her. As she would always be for him.

Jaw tight, she reined in her temper. "And just what is it you want me to tell Fletch to do, Dominique?"

"Why, make the correct decision, of course." With a swivel of her hips, Dominique finally slid off the desktop and back to her spike-heeled feet. "You will do that, won't you, Brenda dear?"

Bren returned the other woman's phony smile. "Absolutely, Dominique. I'll make double sure that he does just that," she promised.

And, she decided furiously as Dominique slinked out of the advertising office, if Fletch so much as looked like he was going to accept his girlfriend's proposal, Bren would chloroform him for his own good, neatly rendering him unconscious until the deadline was past.

In the meantime...

She glanced at the clock and hastily refigured her schedule, scratching from her trade-show lists items that suddenly seemed extremely superfluous. There were far more important things to do now. She not only had to find a dress—something she really did not own and would have to borrow from Sally—and high-heeled shoes, but she also needed time to read some of Sally's book before Fletch showed up at her door that night. Considering he never noticed Bren was anything but a buddy, it was pretty unlikely that he'd ever fall in love with her. Wishing on countless stars hadn't changed the way he looked at her, so one silly self-help book wasn't likely to change the status quo. But if the book could suggest ways in which she might distract him a little, Bren was pretty sure Fletch would realize he'd be making a whopper of a mistake if he married a bimbo like Dominique.

Now all she had to do was a bit of speed-reading and then turn herself into a femme fatale by eight.

Bren groaned out loud this time. She'd never manage it.

True to form, Fletch didn't arrive at Bren's apartment until a quarter to nine. Considering she'd been tapping her foot for forty-five minutes, her greeting was far from warm.

The Freon in her voice didn't bother him, but the sight of her long, shapely legs did. When had they stopped being spindly? he wondered. And when had the rest of her filled out so nicely? The clinging fabric of a black slip dress brushed the top of her knees and draped over very feminine hips and thighs. The tiny straps didn't look strong enough to support the dipping bodice. There were freckles on her pale shoulders, he noticed, and proceeded to follow a particularly fascinating trail of them to the valley between her breasts.

"A person could starve to death waiting for you to show up," Bren growled, swooping up a lacy-looking black shawl and a minuscule, jet-beaded handbag.

Fletch was glad she had her back to him and thus didn't notice when his eyes lingered on her delectable rear end when she bent over.

"I was being considerate," he insisted. "You were so sure you wouldn't get out of the office on time, I thought I'd give you leeway."

"If you were considerate, you would have called to tell me that," Bren said, and pulled him out of her apartment to the parking lot. His low-slung white sports car looked out of place among the age-weary sedans and tiny subcompacts of the other tenants. It looked downright ridiculous parked next to her powder blue, three-quarter-ton truck.

He hadn't met many single women who drove pickups, but because Bren tended to tote all the equipment to their ball games, the truck had always seemed a very appropriate vehicle choice for her.

Until now.

Allowing her to stride ahead of him, Fletch fell back to admire this new Bren. In particular, her enthralling walk. The black pumps she wore were low heeled compared to the type of shoes Dominique favored. They added barely two inches to Bren's willowy height, still allowing him to tower over her, a sensation that made him feel protective.

Something he'd always felt around Bren.

He'd just never associated it with the man-woman thing before. Probably because he had a definite blind spot where Bren was concerned—he just hadn't known it existed until now.

The flirty skirt of her simple dress flipped from side to side as she strode down the path. Afraid that she'd glance back and catch him watching her, Fletch lengthened his stride to come up even with her. He couldn't resist touching her, though, and cupped her elbow with his hand.

Her skin was cool, smooth, soft. The flowery scent of her favorite soap swirled around him, seducing his senses. Fletch inhaled deeply.

"Call you to say I'd be late?" he quipped flippantly. "Naw. You know me too well to expect me to be on time."

"Silly me," Bren murmured sarcastically. "I thought you were desperate enough to do something out of character."

"Who's desperate? I've still got plenty of time."

"Five days and a handful of hours, but who's counting?" Bren said.

"Not me," Fletch insisted, leaning forward to open the passenger-side door for her. "Mind if we keep the top down? It's such a beautiful evening, I hate to waste it."

"Waste the evening or the luxury of a convertible?" Bren asked as she slipped into the car. Her skirt slithered up to display more leg before she brushed the fabric into place, ending his brief show. "Doesn't matter. Knowing you, I came prepared."

While he watched, she draped the lacy scarf around her head and tied it at the nape of her neck. The dangling fringe spilled over her bare shoulders, teasing him with the contrast of dark silk against pale, freckled, satiny flesh.

Fletch was so entranced, he smacked his shin into the rear bumper as he rounded the car.

"Great dress," he said, dropping behind the steering wheel. "How come I've never seen you wear it before?"

"Because the only place I see you outside of work or at Mom's house is at Home-run Harry's Sports Bar after a B and S–sponsored softball game. Can you imagine me wearing a getup like this there?" Bren asked.

He could. And the reaction of the regulars if she ever did. Greyhounds didn't pant as much after a race as the men at Harry's would over Bren in fantasy-inspiring black silk.

"Mmm. On second thought," Fletch murmured as he started the engine, "it is far more sensible to stick with your jeans and team T-shirt." While her jeans hugged her hips nicely, the T-shirt was a giant, shapeless swath of cloth that covered her from collarbone to midthigh without giving a hint of the delightful figure it disguised.

Of course, now that he knew how shapely Bren was, he wondered how many other men had been treated to the sight of her curves. How many had seen her in this little slip of a dress? How many had seen her out of it?

Fletch guided his convertible onto the street and turned toward the interstate. "Ah, I'm not screwing up any plans you might have made with some guy, am I?"

"A little late to worry about that, isn't it?" Bren asked. "But, no, you aren't."

"Sure?" It would be just like her to cancel a date, he knew. Hadn't she done exactly that when he'd needed extra research collected at the library for his marketing paper back in college? Fletch wondered what had ever happened to that guy. Had he ever called Bren back?

"Trust me, slick, there's no one pining away for my company tonight," Bren said.

"Why not?" Fletch demanded. "What's the matter with the guy?"

"There is no guy."

"What do you mean, there is no guy? There has to be a guy."

"No, there doesn't," Bren insisted.

"Sure there does. You're a beautiful woman."

Bren snorted in disbelief.

"You're warm and wonderful," Fletch continued.

"Right."

"Funny."

"Funny as in a good trait to have or funny peculiar?" Bren asked.

"Er, both," Fletch said.

"Thanks. I think."

He maneuvered around a slower vehicle and avoided the freeway entrance ramp. As great as it was to be able to put his foot down on the gas and have the breeze singing through the car, it was impossible to both speed and talk over the sound of the wind. And talking was suddenly far more important, Fletch decided.

"You're what now? Twenty-four?" he asked.

"That's how many candles Mom put on the cake last time," Bren answered. "How old is Dominique?"

"She's . . . hell. Come to think of it, I don't know."

"I'll give you three-to-five odds that she lies about it if you ask her," Bren said.

Fletch glanced over at her, one eyebrow cocked satirically. "Sounds like a sucker bet to me, and I'm no sucker, toots. Besides, I'm too much of a gentleman to ask her how old she is."

"But not enough of one to restrain yourself where I'm concerned. Thanks a million, Layton."

"Considering that I've known you all your life and can handle the simple mathematics involved with our three-year age difference, it was more of a rhetorical question."

"Yeah, yeah," Bren mumbled. She turned to look out the side window, depriving him of the sight of her delicately etched profile. "You think you can talk your way out of anything. Don't pull that bull on me, okay? Save it for strangers," she growled.

Another man might think she was ticked off at him, but Fletch knew it was just an act. Or it was one as far as he was concerned. Their joint history underlined that. When the chips were down, Bren would never turn her back on him.

Although it was turned to him at the moment.

Fletch watched the way the wind tossed her short, dark brown curls despite the restraint of her scarf. When they arrived at the restaurant, chances were her hair would look as if he'd run his fingers through it.

If only he could.

"What's up with you?" Bren asked, swinging back to him.

"I just find it hard to believe that you don't have a boyfriend sitting somewhere sticking pins in a voodoo doll of me," Fletch said.

"Considering I'm not dumb enough to date a guy who's into voodoo, it isn't that hard to believe at all. And if I remember correctly, it isn't my love life that is the subject for discussion tonight, but yours," Bren reminded him.

Fletch wasn't ready to give up, though. "Okay, if not voodoo, is there a guy shelling out money for a hit on me?"

"Yeah, and hit men don't come cheap," Bren snapped. "Now get serious. I've been thinking about things and have decided that all you need to do is consider your feelings for Dominique and—"

"About dinner," Fletch interrupted. "I was considering Italian, but perhaps surf and turf would be a better choice. What do you think, sweetheart?"

Bren frowned at him. "I think you're changing the subject again."

He flashed his raffish smile at her. "You're a tough taskmistress, Brenda Marie Burton. If I promise to talk about Dominique's ultimatum, will you let me do so on a full stomach?"

She looked at him skeptically, but Fletch could see her resolve melting. "You'll consider your feelings?" she asked, still leery.

He was glad she hadn't added Dominique's name to the softly voiced request. Although he knew the time was fast approaching when he would have to make a decision about his erstwhile girlfriend, at the moment he had other priorities.

"Doesn't sound like a very guy thing to do, Bren," Fletch murmured, sidestepping.

"Layton," she moaned, "you make me crazy. This was all your idea. You're the one with personal problems. If you don't—"

"Okay, okay. I swear—" he held up his right hand "—I will delve deeply into my feelings."

"Honestly?" Bren demanded, still suspicious.

"Honestly," he promised.

3

—→ ←—

Day two, continued: The Dinner

The concept that men fall in lust and women in
love is not entirely false. Or entirely true. Strate-
gically, it is best for his mind to be clouded while
yours remains alert.

Land Your Man

The restaurant was dimly lit, the tables linen covered, the food fit for a connoisseur, and the atmo-
sphere reeking of intimacy. A trio played soft jazz in
the background, the drums whispering, the bass
throbbing while a sax moaned sensuously. If Bren
hadn't known better, she would have thought Fletch
was set on seducing her. Of course, now that she was
replete with beef tips in burgundy and had been plied
with wine, Bren had a little difficulty remembering
what her own plan for the evening had been. Something about getting Fletch to face his feelings. Her
handy-dandy book had insisted that it was more than
emotion that made for a long-term, happy mating ex-

perience, but deciding exactly how deeply a person was in love was still a major feature in landing a man.

Not that she wanted to help Dominique land him. But now that she'd calmed down, Bren didn't want to ruin his life if Fletch was passionately attached to the bimbo.

Or rather, Medusa. Boy, had Sally ever pinned the creature correctly.

The chip had slipped off Bren's shoulder as the alcohol worked its wonders, but now it reasserted itself as she recalled every minute of the incident earlier that day. Here she was, prepared to force Fletch to examine his feelings for Dominique, when all the while Medusa lacked a decent attachment to him. The tramp wanted him to marry her for her own self-gratification, for what she would gain materially as his wife.

Fletch leaned across the table and poured another measure of rich, ruby-tinted liquid into Bren's glass. "What about dessert?" he asked. "I saw the cart go by not long ago and it had some wicked-looking pastries on it. I'd go odds on the chance that most of them are cream filled."

Mmm, cream filled. Her weakness. Bren closed her eyes, shutting out the possible sight of such luxury.

"Pass," she said, and opened her eyes to find Fletch signaling for the cart anyway.

"Don't be a martyr," he recommended. "I just realized you lied to me."

"When?"

"About your advanced age."

"I am only twenty-four," Bren insisted. "Still."

"Still," he repeated. "If I recall correctly, your birthday is two days away. Since we'll be in Vegas then, you won't be able to celebrate with your family."

"Like that's a loss," Bren said. "We'll all celebrate when I get back. Mom will insist upon putting twenty-five candles on the cake, thereby putting the smoke alarms on alert."

Fletch grinned lazily at her. "Am I invited to the party?"

"You and the various county fire departments."

The waiter wheeled the dessert extravaganza up to the table. Tiny tarts in ruffled paper cups sat next to small but deadly cakes with fancy icing. A tempting selection of perfectly created ladyfingers drew Bren's eyes.

"Difficult decision, hmm, sweetheart?" Fletch murmured before turning his lethal grin on the waiter. "What would you suggest for a lady with a weakness for both cream filling and chocolate?"

Bren bit back a groan as she was awarded the most sinful-looking bit of pastry on the tray. Fletch opted for tarts and was soon savoring one that was strawberry filled.

"Do you ever listen to me?" Bren asked him.

"When?" Fletch mumbled, his mouth full.

"I said I didn't want dessert."

"Your lips said no but your eyes said yes, yes, yes," he said, swallowing quickly.

Typical male reasoning and inaccurate as hell. Bren glared at him. "What are they saying now?"

"Hmm." He leaned closer. "Let's see. They're glittering. An obvious effect of the excellent company you're keeping."

"*Excellent* would not be among the word choices I'd make," Bren warned.

"Too long a word?" Fletch asked innocently. "But, yes, I do listen to you, sweetheart. It's time to take my feelings in for a review. Right?"

She was a bit surprised that he remembered. "Right," Bren said. "Where would you like to begin?"

Fletch leaned an elbow on the table and rubbed thoughtfully at the faint cleft in his chin.

Despite the fact that she was extremely familiar with every one of his features, Bren found herself staring in fascination at his chin.

At his mouth.

Fletch picked up his napkin and dabbed at the corner of his lips. "Did I get it?" he asked.

"Get what?" Bren demanded, snapping out of her self-induced trance.

"The strawberry goop on my face. I thought that was why you were staring at me."

"Oh, yes, of course. Absolutely. It's gone now," Bren assured him, although there hadn't been any goop on his handsome face. "So…"

"So." Fletch grimaced. "This isn't as easy as I thought it would be. Maybe if you asked me some questions, it would help get the ball rolling. Aren't you going to eat your dessert?"

Bren picked up her fork and sank it into the rich chocolate that covered her eclair. "Well, you've been seeing Dominique for a long time now, which you've got to admit, Fletch, is rare for you."

"Is it?"

"Rocket men don't zip in and out of liaisons as quickly as you used to," Bren said. "Not one of your past relationships was enduring."

He shook his head slightly, the corners of his mouth lifting in amusement. "Wrong."

With pastry balanced on her fork a millimeter from her mouth, Bren froze. "What do you mean, wrong? Dominique is the first woman you've stayed with for any length of time."

"She's the second," he corrected.

"The second?" Bren placed her still-laden fork on the plate. "Someone you saw in college that I don't know about?"

"Nope. Earlier than that."

"High school? No way. I was there, remember? Granted, I was years behind you, but Josh has a big mouth and enjoyed regaling me with both his and your adventures in the back seats of your cars."

"Earlier than high school," Fletch said.

Bren frowned and chewed her bottom lip as she scrolled names from the past through her mind. At last she shook her head. "No one. I considered Barbara Aram, but you were juggling Nancy West and Juliet Weingarten as well, so—"

Fletch pushed back his chair and stood up. "Listen to that music," he murmured. "Let's dance."

"Dance?" Bren glanced toward the bandstand. Toward the minuscule—and empty—dance floor.

"Yeah, dance. You don't still want to lead, do you? I warn you, any arm wrestling done to determine who gets to lead will see me the winner," Fletch said.

Feeling like she was in a dream, Bren got to her feet. "But there's no one else dancing."

His fingers wove intimately with hers. "Their loss," he said, tugging her toward the postage-stamp-size dance floor.

"It's a slow dance," Bren noted, still reluctant.

"Afraid I'll step on your toes?"

Oh, she was afraid all right, but not of that. When Fletch slid his arm around her, drawing her close to his own body, Bren felt weak.

His cheek slid against hers, the sensation both rough and smooth.

"Mmm, just the right size," he murmured near her ear. His breath stirred her curls and set off a series of land mines she hadn't known had been laid.

"What is?" she whispered, staring resolutely at the neat Windsor knot of his tie.

"You are," Fletch said. "Your height. I don't have to bend over you as I would with a shorter woman."

"I always wanted to be petite," Bren confessed.

"Mmm, no. You're perfect as is."

Now why hadn't any man she dated ever told her that? Bren wondered. And why did it have to be Fletch who tossed the compliment, rather like it was a bone, to her? He wasn't her lover. He was her best friend.

Swaying in his arms, she found it hard to remember that's all he was.

"So, who was the first female you had a long-standing relationship with?" Bren asked. "Your mom?"

"Hmm. I didn't think about her," Fletch said.

She glanced up at him in surprise. "You didn't? Then who...?"

The smile began in his dark eyes, warming them in a way that had Bren's solar plexus acting extremely flighty. When it curved his lips, the effect was downright deadly.

"It's you, Bren," Fletch murmured, drawing her more securely into his arms. "Who else but you?"

Her saucer-size eyes widened with surprise at the announcement. Fletch decided to take advantage of the moment and slid his hand up her spine until it rested on warm, bare skin between her shoulder blades.

"Dip?" he asked, and bent her back quickly before Bren had regained her senses. Her arm slipped around his neck, her grip tightening as she tried to keep her balance. Her wild, corkscrew curls tossed in attractive disarray—well, further disarray, he noted with pleasure. They had remained tousled from the drive to the restaurant with the top down. Bren hadn't even realized it, either. Dominique, he knew, would not only have insisted that he convert the convertible to sedan status, but the moment they arrived at the restaurant would have whisked her delectable form to the powder room to ensure her hair and makeup remained perfect. Thank God Bren was a natural.

She was, however, frowning at him. "Cute, Layton. What comes next? Overhead lifts?"

Fletch righted her, enjoying the way Bren's body plastered itself to his as she clung a moment longer, her breasts flattened against his chest, her nose even with his before she dropped down off her toes. Balance regained, she forced space between them, but he still felt a bit dizzy from the contact. He wondered if Bren was as aware of him as he was of her.

Her pretty green eyes had narrowed and were spitting mad as she glared at him.

Apparently not.

"What do you mean, your relationship with me predates the Dominique affair?" Bren snapped. "You and I don't have the same type of relationship."

"Now why is that, do you think?" Fletch asked. When he tightened his grip at her waist, Bren's brows merged together over her nose.

A delightfully tilted nose.

Bren blinked. "What?"

"Why do you think we've never—"

She didn't let him finish. "You're stalling again, Layton," she snapped.

Fletch was pleased to note she was blushing, though.

"Don't you dare dip me again," Bren warned.

"Then stop pulling away," Fletch said. "I dance far better when I'm close to my partner."

"Well, I prefer to be able to breathe and dance at the same time," Bren said, resisting. "Now, about Dominique."

He groaned faintly. "Must we talk about her?" He rubbed his cheek against Bren's curls. They were soft, bouncy and intoxicating. Not a hint of mousse or hair spray to deter a man's exploration. He nuzzled the area just above her ear, breathing in her scent. It was more than just soap and the borrowed smell of some flower. It was pure woman. Pure Bren.

She leaned back in his arms. "We have to talk about Dominique. That's why we're having dinner together."

"We've had dinner. We're past that part of the evening," Fletch said.

The music ended. There was a twitter of applause for the musicians. Bren stepped out of his arms, tossed an appreciative grin toward the men on the bandstand and turned back to their table.

Fletch snagged her wrist and swung her back in place. "How many slow songs do you guys know?" he called to the saxophone player.

"Oh, at least another twenty minutes' worth," the man answered. He turned to the two musicians behind him. "Right, guys?"

A couple of twenties flowed from Fletch's fingers to the sax man's hand. "Think you could play some of them twice?" he asked.

The bills disappeared. "No problem." A moment later, the drummer was dusting his drums, the bass was throbbing and the sax was moaning softly again.

Fletch swayed to the music, enjoying the brush of Bren's body against his. "Now, where were we? Ah, I remember." He buried his nose in her sweet-smelling hair.

Bren sighed with disgust. "This isn't going to work, Fletch."

"It's working wonderfully. Slow dancing is so relaxing. With all the stress we've been through getting ready for the toothpaste promotion, we both need a break," he said. "Aren't you enjoying yourself?"

Her lashes dipped over her eyes, shielding them from him. "Yes, but—"

"If I promise to talk about Dominique on the plane tomorrow, will you drop the subject and enjoy yourself?" he asked. "We've got at least five hours in the air. That's pretty much uninterrupted time, Bren."

She hesitated, then capitulated. "Oh, all right. I know I'm going to hate myself for agreeing, but—"

Fletch rewarded her with a light brush of his lips at her hairline. Or perhaps he was rewarding himself, he thought. He'd wanted to kiss her, taste her, ever since he'd arrived at her apartment to find she had metamorphosed into a beautiful woman. Or had the longing been with him earlier, during that far-from-satisfying lunch in the park?

He still had a hard time believing this was Bren. Cute, boyish Bren. The girl-next-door in appearance as well as in real life. The antithesis of Dominique.

And she was affecting him the same way that Dominique did.

No. Differently. Yet...

At last accepting the situation and relaxing, Bren snuggled against him.

Fletch hugged her closer. "This is nice," he said, resting his cheek against her hair. "You're a good dancer."

Bren chuckled softly. "You're only saying that because I haven't tried to lead."

"Maybe."

"It's a long time since we danced together," she murmured.

"Ten years?"

"Longer. I was the only available partner for you and Josh to practice with before you went to your first dance," Bren said.

Fletch nodded at the reminder. "Gosh, junior high. Boy, was I awkward back then."

"You?" She tilted her head back and smiled up at him. "I find that hard to believe. You were born cocky."

With another woman he would have played up the double entendre. Fletch let it slide by. This was Bren, not some floozy like...

Like Dominique.

Huh.

"Naw," he drawled. "It's all an act. I'm constantly scared sh—"

"I get the idea, slick," Bren said. "And I don't believe it for a minute. Remember, I've been a victim of your charm time and again."

"My charm?" Fletch grinned widely.

"Well, perhaps *charm* is a little inaccurate, but it's the most polite word I could think of for *bull*."

"Bull," he repeated, a bit deflated. "Careful. My ego is a delicate thing, sweetheart."

She actually giggled. "Right. Tell me another one, Layton. Mmm. You know, this really is relaxing. Either that or the wine has made me numb."

He could think of a number of things that would be even more relaxing—after a time—and infinitely more satisfying than dancing. There was just one problem.

This was Bren. He couldn't treat his best friend as callously as he had other women. Even if he was more aware of Bren as a desirable woman than he'd ever been with those others.

"Do you love her?" Bren asked softly. Reluctantly, he thought.

Fletch decided to play dumb. "Who?"

"Dominique."

"I . . ." His throat grew tight and he had to clear it before continuing. "I don't know. Remember? That's what we're going to talk about tomorrow. I'm too cheap to pay a shrink to pull the information out of me, so I'm bugging you instead."

"That's what friends are for," Bren assured him.

He'd been teasing. Kidding. But Bren had been serious.

Damn. Double damn.

She was right on the money, too. That was exactly what friends were for. They were there when you needed them, willing to do whatever it took to help you out of a mess.

Which was what he was in at the moment.

"I don't deserve you, you know that?" Fletch asked.

"Yeah," Bren said with a quick, impish grin. "I know that."

"What have I ever done for you, Bren? Truthfully."

"You're serious? Lots of things, Fletch."

"Name one."

She didn't even pause to think, which surprised him greatly. "You got me the job at Bailey and Salazar."

He brushed that off. "You were qualified for the job and landed it yourself. All I did is tell you there was an opening."

Bren wasn't discouraged, though. "You made sure I was involved in the Fresh All Day kickoff. That's a great thing to add to my résumé and—"

He dipped her again without warning her first, simply to get her to stop granting him sainthood. Bren didn't gripe about the move this time. She just held on tight.

"I didn't arrange it, Bren. You were the best person for the job," Fletch explained, righting her again.

"Okay, but you did—"

He sighed deeply. "Bet I didn't. Why do you put up with me? I haven't done anything to deserve your friendship. Not one damn thing."

"Don't be ridiculous," Bren exclaimed. "How could I not be there when you need me? You were my hero when we were kids."

"When we were kids. Not now, huh?" The evening was turning downright depressing. Fletch looked off across the restaurant at the couples seated at tables. One pair had taken courage and joined Bren and him on the dance floor, but most were merely seated close together, their heads bent toward each other, effectively blocking out the rest of the world.

Suddenly he was jealous of those small worlds. Wanted one of his own.

With Bren.

It would never happen. He'd treated her too badly to ever have a shot at it.

Bren's fingertips caressed his cheek, bringing his eyes back to hers. "You're still my hero," she whispered. "Nothing will ever change that."

"Not even Dominique?" Fletch asked.

Bren shook her head lightly, her delightful curls quivering, begging to be touched. "Not even her," she promised. "Once you love someone, you—"

Oops! Bren bit down on her tongue to keep it from making another slip.

The wattage of Fletch's grin had increased a hundredfold when he looked down at her. "Love?" he echoed.

There was no way she was going to slide out of it, Bren realized. "Of course love," she said. "Why wouldn't I love you, considering we have such a long shared history? However, there's love and there's being in love. Two very different states."

"You sure?" he asked, his nearness making Bren question her own statement.

"Trust me," she insisted. "For instance, you don't feel about Dominique the same way you do about me, right?"

"I've never felt about Dominique as I do about you," Fletch murmured into her hair.

"See? Case closed." Just to play it safe, Bren turned her face away from his, her cheek brushing against the lapel of his jacket.

"Of course," Fletch continued, "I haven't known Dominique nearly as long. Do you think growing old together will give us the same kind of relationship that growing up together has given you and me?''

"Maybe," Bren said, although she didn't believe Dominique was capable of being anyone's friend, which was basically the only type of relationship she herself had with Fletch.

"I can't exactly picture Dominique sitting in the rocking chair next to mine at the retirement home," Fletch admitted. "Think that means I'll outlive her?"

If Dominique was missing from the picture, Bren knew why. The bimbo had run off with another man, one with more bucks than Fletch. It wasn't exactly the type of thing even a friend pointed out to a besotted man, though.

"Maybe she's just off having another face-lift," Bren suggested instead.

"Good point," Fletch agreed, silently deciding Dominique would have left him at the first hint that he intended to move into a retirement community. Provided, that is, he married her.

Thinking about Dominique's ultimatum put a real damper on his spirits. He'd looked forward to this evening with Bren because they always had a good time together. Lots of good times together.

In a way, it was amazing that he could say that of a woman and not have sex in mind.

It was most definitely on his mind now.

"What do you say to rocking into senility with me?" Fletch asked.

"Too late. You're already there," Bren quipped. "Besides, I'll be on the shuffleboard court. No tame rocking chairs for me. When Josh's kids come to visit me, you can direct them there."

The music cruised to a stop again. This time, after clapping appreciatively, Bren didn't make a break for the table. Fletch was glad. He liked having her stand so near and yet not touch him. It let his imagination run rampant. It was in full gallop when he realized what she had said.

"What do you mean, Josh's kids? What about your own?"

Bren glanced at him over her shoulder.

That creamy, satiny, freckled, bare shoulder.

"Oh, I probably won't have any," she said.

"Sure you will. Once some guy sweeps you off your feet—"

Bren laughed. "Guys," she insisted, "don't know I exist. Other than as a competent shortstop on their ball team or as a handy gofer."

Fletch was scandalized. "They make you make coffee?"

"Oh, no. I'm one of them, you know? It's the wanna-be Dominiques who handle coffee duties."

"Come on. You date. Don't you?"

"Occasionally. Briefly, usually."

The band swung into a new tune, but it wasn't until Bren moved back into his arms that Fletch realized it. He took both her hands and directed them around his neck so that he had an excellent excuse to slide his own arms completely around her.

"Why's that? I happen to think you look nice," he said. Better than nice. It wasn't a good time to tell her that, though.

"Ah," Bren cooed. "Nice. A killer word. You know men don't date *nice* girls. Heck, you're a perfect example of that, Fletch, so I shouldn't have to explain it to you."

He stared at her. "I'm lost."

"I've never met a single man who dated because he was looking for a life's mate. More like a single night's mate."

Seeing red at the thought of some dolt using Bren, Fletch glared down at her. "Who was he?" he demanded. "I'll—"

Bren leaned back in his embrace. "Excuse me? Why do I hear echoes of prom night here? I can handle myself. I don't need a big brother."

"Hell, your own brother is useless," Fletch growled. "If it was up to him, you would have been grappling in a back seat with that no-neck date you had for the prom."

"*Tsk, tsk,*" Bren murmured. "All these years I've been blaming him for ruining my life when all along it was you."

More couples were joining them on the dance floor now. One cheerful pair whirled by, demonstrating steps learned in a ballroom-dancing class. The woman's gown whirled as her escort spun her.

Fletch glanced briefly at her legs and decided Bren's were far better—long, shapely, and his particular weakness where women were concerned.

Was that because he'd spent his early life scrambling up hills and trees a breath behind Bren? She'd always had wonderfully long legs, although they'd been gangly more than shapely back then. Time had cured that failing very nicely. Very nicely indeed.

Bren watched as her dance partner ogled another woman. Well, what did she expect? He was susceptible to beautiful women. Always had been. Always would be.

It was time she boarded her pumpkin coach and returned to real life. Even Cinderella hadn't been able to extend her fantasy beyond midnight.

"It's getting late, Fletch," Bren said. "And we've got an early flight to catch tomorrow. Can we call it a night?"

"What? Oh, sure. Shall I pick you up in the morning?" he asked.

Bren's curls tossed. "No, I'd prefer not to miss the plane. How about if I pick you up? And call you to get you out of bed, too?"

Fletch thought about how much more convenient it would be if she woke up in his bed, but figured Bren would black his eye if he suggested it.

"Oh ye of little faith," he murmured. "Okay, we'll leave at the end of this song. You know, we really should do this again. I've had a great time. How about you?"

"Mmm," she agreed. "It's been lovely."

"I'm glad you enjoyed yourself, Bren," Fletch said and, giving in to temptation, kissed her cheek. If he lingered over the job a little more than mere friendship might have indicated was proper, he figured his reckless reputation could take the heat for the slip in protocol.

To hell with protocol. She tasted great. It would be even better when he could kiss her properly. But doing so took a little more courage than he had at the moment.

And that was one hell of a sobering realization. Him! Afraid to kiss a woman! Often his lips had been locked to a woman's before he knew her last name. Sometimes even before he knew her first name.

But this time was different. This time it was Bren he wanted to kiss.

At the gentle brush of his lips, color rushed into Bren's face. "Thanks," she mumbled, fighting down an urge to never wash her cheek again. Fletch had kissed her in the past, but always a brotherly smack on the forehead, never this tender, all-too-sensuous caress.

He nuzzled his cheek against hers. "My pleasure," he murmured.

He was wrong. It had been all hers. He could never know that, though.

Clamping down on a soft purr of contentment, Bren allowed herself to rub her face against his, as if by accident, as they danced.

The move coincided with one of his, bringing their mouths within a breath of each other. Bren felt as if every nerve in her body had gone on alert. She waited, wondering if he would kiss her. Really kiss her.

Fletch smiled tenderly down at her and swung her away in a slow twirl. When he guided her back into his arms, there was more distance between them than there had been moments before.

Reality had the consistency of a ton of bricks being dumped on her hopes, squashing them flat.

Bren gave herself a mental shake. It was the music. The wine. No doubt he'd forgotten who he was with. At the touch of his lips against her cheek, her heart had leapt to her throat. Now it lay heavily in the pit of her stomach. She was doomed to dream, that's all there was to it. Not only was she one of the guys, his buddy, his best friend, she was the damned *nice* girl. There wasn't a chance in hell Fletch would ever notice she was as female as Dominique. Well, not as overtly female, but female all the same.

Bren filed the sensation of the tender kiss away. It was really too bad he'd probably be married by next Monday. She could really get used to evenings in his arms.

4

Day three: Tuesday

By now your man has become more attentive to
you, even demonstrating affection through a minor physical act such as holding your hand or
simply showing a preference for your company.
It is time to step up your campaign.

Land Your Man

After a night of tossing and turning, and an imagination that had gone wild—erotically wild—Bren
heard her alarm go off. She was even more vehement
in quieting it than usual.

Dawn was breaking outside her window. A host of
birds were busy gossiping in the trees. Probably about
her, Bren thought. About how incredibly stupid she
had been the night before. She should have resisted
when Fletch wanted her to dance with him. Each song
had brought them closer together, inadvertently rubbing against each other. Well, inadvertently on his
part. She'd been indulging in a million daydreams.

Stupid, that's what she'd been.

At least Fletch was equally stupid. He hadn't tumbled to what she'd been doing. He had just seen his buddy Bren, not a female in heat. Not even after that incredibly tender kiss.

Why had he done it? Had it simply been the wine and the music? Or had he kissed her because she'd followed the advice in Sally's book in borrowing a dress that looked a lot like expensive lingerie?

Ooh! That damned book! Bren groaned and pulled her pillow over her head.

She didn't have time to waste, though. Still clutching the pillow to her breast, she rolled over and reached for the phone.

Fletch answered on the first ring. "Good morning, sweetheart," he greeted her cheerfully.

Bren frowned. "It's me," she said. "Not Dominique."

"Oh, I know," he assured her even more brightly.

Cheerful and bright! Fletch was never either in the morning. This was obviously an alien being.

"Sleep well?" he asked.

"As well as could be expected." After an evening of undiluted Fletch Layton charm, she added silently. Which was to say not at all. "Can you be ready in half an hour?"

"I'm already ready," he said. "I'll make a quick stop at the doughnut shop and come pick you up. You take your coffee with two sugars, right?"

Bren stared at the receiver. "Who are you and what have you done with Fletcher Layton?" she asked.

He chuckled. "Hey, I can be as considerate as the next guy."

"You can?"

"Shall I prove it to you?" he asked.

"Don't put yourself to the trouble," Bren said. "Just remember we need to be at the airport within the hour. I know I'm going to hate myself for saying this, but yes, it does make sense for you to pick me up, since you're ready. Just don't get sidetracked on your way here."

"Aye, aye, Capt'n," Fletch said.

Bren could almost see him saluting. He'd probably done it with the wrong hand.

"Just one question," he added. "Chocolate, caramel or jelly filled?"

"Huh?"

"Doughnut preference, darling."

Bren nearly dropped the phone. Darling?

"Ah..."

"All three? Excellent choice. I'll be there in twenty minutes at the latest."

Bren was still staring at the receiver when the dial tone sounded.

She was dew-drenched and delightful when she answered his jaunty rap on her front door. Her chestnut curls were tight and sopping wet. The rest of her was probably glowing and damp, too, he figured, but considering the white, terry-cloth robe she wore enveloped her from neck to ankle, he could only fantasize about how she looked beneath it.

"Mmm. You're like a nymph who's just stepped from beneath an enchanted waterfall," Fletch said, his gaze slipping from her still-dripping hair to the bare toes visible below the hem of her robe. Unlike Dominique's, Bren's toenails weren't painted poppy red. They weren't painted at all.

Bren turned away from the door and padded across the living room. "Can it, Layton," she advised. "Let me throw on some clothes and we can be on our way."

Yep, Bren was nothing like Dominique.

Thank God.

Fletch trailed after her. "Hey, have breakfast first. Don't mind me. I happen to love sitting across the table from nearly naked women."

Bren stopped in the doorway and scowled back at him.

"Okay. How about your coffee will get cold if you don't drink it now?" he suggested.

"I'll be back in two minutes," she said, and disappeared.

Two minutes. Right. There wasn't a woman alive who could get dressed in under half an hour. An hour or longer in some cases.

When Bren strode into the kitchen barely a hundred seconds later, he nearly choked on his coffee.

She'd followed his lead, Fletch noticed, and wore jeans and a conservatively cut blouse tucked into the waistband. The blouse was the same color green as her eyes and of a clingy silk fabric that made it quite apparent she had been hiding her light under a bushel basket—or under shapeless, oversize clothing—in the past. While her sexy little dress the evening before had given him a healthy appreciation of her charms, it hadn't displayed her narrow waist or lushly curved hips. The jeans did that and more this morning.

Feeling his throat grow dry, Fletch hastily gulped at his coffee and burned his tongue.

Bren didn't notice. For which he was glad. Her attention was turned to the pastries in the box he'd placed in the center of her table.

"You really expect me to eat half a dozen doughnuts?" she asked, her voice ringing with the hard-edged sarcasm he had come to associate with her. It had softened briefly the night before. When she'd been held close in his arms. "I don't know where you get the idea that I'm insatiable."

Fletch perked up. "Insatiable?" he echoed, wiggling his eyebrows.

"For sweets," she said. "You can stop the Groucho impressions now. You know..." Bren helped herself to a pastry drenched in caramel icing, placed it on the napkin before her and licked at her now sticky fingers.

He watched her, hoping she didn't hear when he swallowed loudly. Dominique had licked her fingers like that, too, he remembered, but she'd also pinned him with a hot, suggestive glance while she did so. Bren hadn't the slightest idea what she was doing to him. Couldn't know, since she wasn't looking at him, but at the rest of the doughnuts, making a second choice.

"We really should take my truck rather than your convertible to the airport," she said. "Not only will the luggage fit in the camper bed better..."

Bed, Fletch thought. Oh, yes, a bed and Bren in it.

"We'll be gone for the best part of a week and your car would be too much of a temptation to car thieves," she continued.

Temptation. That's what she was all right. The sweetest, most innocent kind.

"Why aren't you eating, Fletch? Considering you're the one who insisted on breakfast, I thought you were starving."

He was, he was. Just not for food.

And it was bound to get worse as the day went on. He'd be sitting next to her in the cramped confines of a plane, his knee brushing hers every time one of them shifted position.

There were a good many positions he'd pictured them in together during the past sleepless night. Some flashed in erotic detail through his mind once more.

Without tasting it, he finished off his doughnut, washing it down with equally tasteless coffee.

"What do you think?" Bren asked.

She really didn't want to know that. Fletch quickly reviewed what she'd said rather than concentrate on the delightful tangents his own mind had followed.

"You're right," he said. "There isn't much trunk space in the convertible. While you finish getting ready, I'll take your luggage out and transfer mine over."

Bren fished in her jeans pocket and tossed her keys to him. "Oh, all I have to do yet is slip on some shoes. I'll bring my own stuff out while you move your bags into the truck."

Just slip on shoes? He glanced down at her feet. She had pulled on cotton socks so he couldn't see her polish-free toes. There wasn't a speck of makeup on her pretty face. No mascara, no blusher. Her curls were still damp and tousled.

Noticing the direction of his gaze, Bren raised a hand to her hair, running her fingers through the tight, copper-tinted corkscrews. "My hair will dry en route, if that's what you're wondering," she said.

Actually, he'd been wondering what it would feel like to bury his fingers in the clinging, wet mass. How she'd react if he did. If he tilted her face up and...

"Fletch?"

He snapped out of the pleasant daydream. "Oh. Sorry. Guess I'm not as awake as I thought. Want another doughnut?"

"I've already had two," she said. "You're the one who's fallen behind. Finish up so we can get on the road. Should we take the rest of these along for the guys?"

Guys. Good lord! She was right. She was the only woman being sent to Vegas. The rest of the Bailey and Salazar team consisted of a debonair junior sales rep, a public-relations hunk and a former bodybuilder from advertising. Every one of them had been chosen for the Fresh All Day team because they were not only qualified but were young, attractive, outgoing and had dazzling dental work.

And when the "guys" caught sight of Bren, dressed as Fletch had never seen Bren dressed before, there was going to be hell to pay.

"Naw. Let them get their own pastries," he growled. And if they even looked like they were interested in his pastry—Bren—heaven help them.

* * *

Normally, Bren loved living in southwestern Ohio. But whenever she traveled and couldn't get a direct flight to anywhere—which usually happened—she had to admit there were probably more convenient places to live.

The flight to Chicago for the connection to Las Vegas had gone without a hitch. Not only had she and Fletch arrived within the thirty-minute envelope prior to takeoff, so had Mick, Kurt and Steve. The foul-up occurred less than an hour after they left Chicago.

Next to her, Fletch was faking sleep to avoid talking about Dominique once more. Earlier he'd used the brevity of the hop to the Windy City as an excuse to put it off, then the fact that drinks were being served by the stewardesses. He now had less than five days left before committing himself to marriage with his girlfriend, and only Bren seemed conscious of the incessant ticking of the clock. Rather than face his future head-on, Fletch was finding all manner of things to talk about—none of them even vaguely related to Dominique.

Bren was considering kicking him in the shin to end his current blindness when the aircraft intercom crackled to life.

"Ladies and gentlemen, I'm sorry, but the captain tells me we are experiencing a slight mechanical difficulty with the aircraft and, rather than continue our flight to Las Vegas at this time, we will be landing shortly. He has called ahead requesting that a different plane be readied, but we are expecting a delay of an hour or more before it is available. We would appreciate your understanding and patience."

Fletch continued to play possum, so Bren elbowed him. "Wake up. The plane is going down. You've got ten seconds tops to make your peace with a higher power."

He yawned and straightened in his seat. "I'm not calling Dominique, no matter what," he grumbled.

"Ladies and gentlemen, the captain has turned on the seat-belt sign. We request at this time that you straighten your seat backs and prepare for landing," the voice on the intercom said calmly.

Fletch looked over at Bren. "I thought you said we were crashing."

"I lied and you know it. But speaking of Dominique..."

"Yeah, she and plane crashes have a lot in common," he agreed.

"You've been putting off doing the right thing long enough," Bren insisted. "Last night you told me you didn't know if you loved her, but you didn't say how you feel when you're with her. Or when you aren't with her. For instance, do you miss her right this minute?"

"Hell, no," Fletch said. "She'd be railing at me about putting her on a plane with mechanical difficulties. Not exactly a dulcet sound, if you know what I mean."

"If we were indeed facing our last minutes on earth..."

"You're awfully damn taken with this crashing bit," he grumbled. "Been thinking about your own last minutes on earth, Bren? What kind of life is passing before your eyes? A good one? No, don't answer that one. Of course it's been good. But, more importantly, do you have any regrets over things you haven't done?"

"Fasten your seat belt," Bren recommended. "Why would I have any regrets? I've done everything anyone could expect to do in nearly twenty-five years." She turned to stare out the window. Clouds obstructed the view. The plane hit an air pocket and bucked a bit, shivering with the turbulence.

"Everything?" Fletch echoed. "Some women have children by your advanced age."

"Some women have their children at a much more advanced age, too," Bren countered. "Besides, I'm not going to be a mother, remember? I'm aiming for favorite-aunt status."

"You could be both."

Bren gave him a long look. Fletch squirmed uneasily in his seat.

"Dominique," she said. "At this very moment do you miss her?"

Fletch squared his shoulders and gazed directly into Bren's eyes. "No," he said. "When I'm with you, I don't even think about her."

"I noticed," Bren murmured, her tone far from complimentary.

"Hey, I'm being truthful. Isn't that what you wanted?" he whined. He hated himself for doing it, but what was a guy to do when cornered? Lie, maybe?

He couldn't do that to Bren. Not outright, at least.

"Have you ever been in love?" Fletch demanded, counterattacking. "Because if you haven't, it could be that you have no idea how it feels to be in love and therefore might, just might, not be the best person to help me work this through. Not that I'm planning on finding someone else to tal—"

"I have been," Bren said.

"—Talk to, but . . . what did you say?"

"I said I've been in love, so you don't need to fret about my qualifications as your unofficial shrink," Bren said.

Fletch looked at her, his expression that of a man who'd just had the rug pulled out from beneath him. "What do you mean, you've been in love?"

"Seems pretty cut-and-dried to me," Bren insisted. "You asked if I'd ever been and I said yes I had. We move on. Now, when you look at Dominique—"

"When?" Fletch snapped.

"When what?"

"When did you fall in love?"

"Oh, it was a while ago," Bren said. "Does Dominique make your stomach feel all fluttery?"

"Actually, oysters do. Who was he?"

"Who was who?"

"The guy you fell in love with. Do I know him?"

The plane dipped a little farther into the clouds. A flash of lightning briefly lit the cabin. Bren looked out into the storm. "You aren't going to get me off the subject, Fletch. And the subject, as you seem to keep forgetting, is your future with Dominique."

"So I do know him," Fletch murmured. He turned to glance over at where Mick, Kurt and Steve sat. Was it one of them? Someone from the company softball team? Bren had been awfully buddy-buddy with some of the guys at those after-game drinking fests at the sports bar. Some of the men had even draped their arms around her shoulders as they joked with her.

Bren punched him in the arm. Hard.

"Ouch." Fletch rubbed his bicep. "What was that for?"

"Everything!" she snarled. "You are driving me nuts. First you say you want my help, then you change the subject from your love life to my lack of one. Mine is not the problem. Yours is."

"Not if you have a lack of one," Fletch insisted. "That's an even bigger problem. Let's talk about why there is no romance in your life. What happened to that guy you were in love with?"

Bren gritted her teeth and growled. On the arms of her chair, her fingers curled into claws.

Fletch decided it would be physically safer for him at the moment to shut up. Was it air travel or memories of her mysterious former lover that had turned Bren rabid? He frowned, running through a mental catalog of men who might have done her wrong, and found his fingers naturally folding into fists as the faces flashed by.

Rain began pelting the window and the plane bounced in for a landing.

"The captain has informed me we will have a delay of approximately two hours before a new plane will be available, ladies and gentlemen," the cabin attendant purred soothingly over the intercom, once the plane approached the gate. "We ask that you deplane. For those of you wishing to look for other connections, the—"

Fletch reached across the aisle and nudged Mick's arm. "What do you guys say we drown our layover sorrows at the nearest cocktail lounge?"

"Sounds good to me," the public-relations man said as the plane glided to a stop.

Fletch flicked his seat belt open and stretched to his feet. "Great. Last one there pays," he announced and slipped quickly up the aisle.

Mick fished in his trouser pocket for his money clip and peeled off bills. The bartender scooped them up and returned to the far end of the bar to watch an old "Columbo" rerun on the TV set there.

"What happened to Bren?" Mick asked, glancing out to the concourse. "Isn't she joining us?"

"You only asking because you had to pick up the tab?" Fletch asked.

Steve shook his head. "No, he isn't. He's got the hots for her."

Fletch's hand froze, his glass suspended three inches from his nose.

Mick picked up his own draft beer. "So what good does that do me? She doesn't know I'm alive."

"Don't take it seriously, man," Kurt murmured, staring remorsefully into his own beer. "She's never noticed that half the male staff in advertising watch her every move."

"Half the male staff?" Fletch repeated, his voice sounding strangely strained to his ears.

"Rampant lust, and she acts as if she doesn't know it exists," Kurt said.

"It's not an act. Bren is so innocent, she hasn't the least idea that she drives us crazy," Mick explained.

"Bren?" Fletch croaked. Granted, he'd been overly aware of her himself lately, but he hadn't realized there was an epidemic in progress where she was concerned.

"Hey, we don't expect you to understand," Kurt assured Fletch. "You've got that stacked chick hanging on your every word."

Considering the wording of Dominique's nasty little note, Fletch nearly didn't recognize her as the "stacked chick" who hung on his every word.

"What's really frustrating is that Bren isn't giving us the cold shoulder. She honestly doesn't realize any of us are interested in...well, in a far-from-businesslike relationship with her," Steve said.

"Damn, but that's attractive in a woman." Mick sighed. "You know that beige getup she had on yesterday?"

"Yeah?" Fletch asked, leaning forward.

"Drives me wild," Mick confessed. "It covers her from the neck on down and my mind spends a good part of the day fantasizing about what she looks like under all that cloth."

"Oh, yeah. It clung just enough to fuel my dreams," Steve agreed. He stared off into space, his gaze slightly besotted.

"Once," Kurt said, lowering his voice, "she took the jacket off while she was working."

"Bending over the drawing table?" Mick asked hopefully.

"Way over it," Kurt answered.

Mick groaned. "You're killing me."

Fletch looked at each of them in turn and shook his head. "Did any of you actually ask her out?"

"I tried once," Kurt said. "I said, 'Bren? I've got tickets to the Reds game and I was wondering if—' and she didn't let me get any further."

"Turned down a chance to see the Reds play?" Fletch demanded. "Can't be. She loves baseball."

Kurt took a fortifying draft of beer. "Don't I know it. Not many girls—"

"Women," Fletch corrected. "Believe me, after being put through one of those politically correct management workshops, I know better than to call them *girls*. At least where they might overhear you."

"Well, not many *women* are as enthusiastic about baseball or other sporting events as Bren is. I thought I was home free waving those tickets under her nose," Kurt said.

"So what happened?" Fletch asked.

"She tossed me one of those casual grins—"

"Impish," Mick said.

"Devastating," Steve insisted.

"—And she said, 'Don't forget to take your glove with you when you go so those fly balls home right to you, Kurt.' Then she asked me some question about box design on laundry detergent and I lost my nerve," he murmured.

Mick and Steve commiserated with him.

"She hasn't a clue," Steve said. "She sees us as buddies, not guys. You know how that is, Layton. She treats you even worse."

"Yeah," Kurt agreed. "Like you were a eunuch."

Fletch nearly choked on his beer. "A—a what?"

"You know. Harmless. She touches you," Mick said. "I've watched her."

"You mean when she slugged me a little while ago on the plane?" Fletch asked, rubbing his arm in remembrance.

"That and those caresses."

Fletch's throat went dry.

"Oh, yeah," Steve agreed with longing. "Her hand on your knee, on your arm. The way she leans over you when she wants your attention."

"She only does those things with you, man," Kurt said. "Probably because she's known you forever."

"And that's why she considers you a eunuch," Mick insisted. "I wouldn't trade places with you for the world, Layton. Not for the world."

Bren lingered in her seat and watched her male associates nearly trample their fellow passengers in their rush to get off the plane. *Men,* she fumed silently. What were they, other than practically worthless beings? Why had she befriended so many of them in the past? She was a sadist, that's why. Some latent part of her personality enjoyed being frustrated. That had to be it. There was really no other reason why a reasonably intelligent woman like herself associated with such sad specimens of humanity.

From now on, Bren swore, she'd go out of her way to make friends among the females of the species. Women like Sally, who were up-front and honest and...

Drat. As fond as she was of her soon-to-be sister-in-law, Sally had confessed to using tricks to get Josh altar-bound. She'd used *Land Your Man* although she'd kept that news from Josh himself. So Sally wasn't up-front or honest in her dealings. She was manipulative. Perhaps not as flagrant as Dominique, but...

Bren sighed deeply. Dominique wasn't a prime example of modern womanhood, either, unless a person counted looking like she'd slinked off a men's fantasy calendar as a plus.

Obviously, in order to ferret out new friends, Bren thought, she was going to have to go much farther afield than she had in the past.

Either that or make do with the flawed friends she already had.

And speaking of flawed friends, she was going to have to formulate a new plan for getting her erstwhile best friend to make up his mind about Dominique. If he didn't soon, she'd probably try to throttle him, she was that exasperated with him.

Bren gathered up her duffel-bag-size purse and followed the last of the passengers off the plane. Being the last of the B and S team to arrive at the cocktail lounge would mean she had to pick up the tab, so Bren bypassed the bar and headed for the newsstand. She'd just begun to leaf through her third magazine when Fletch materialized at her elbow.

"Get lost?" he asked.

"Excellent idea," Bren said, not bothering to look up from the magazine. "Why don't you get lost?"

"Still mad at me, hmm?"

Bren flipped over another page and ignored him.

"Don't do this to me, Bren," Fletch pleaded.

"Do what?" she murmured, faking an interest in an article on tourism in Pakistan.

"Turn female on me," Fletch said.

The magazine snapped closed. Bren's lips thinned in anger. "What did you say?" she snarled.

"You know what I mean. The dreaded silent treatment. You usually don't sink that low," he insisted.

Bren dropped the magazine back in the rack and turned on her heel. "The ice is getting thinner by the minute, Layton. If I were you, I'd turn in my skates before it's too late."

"Bren."

She kept walking, temper rising by the minute.

He was right on her heels. "Bren."

She wheeled on him, causing Fletch to jerk to a halt to keep from running into her. "Stay away from me, Layton. I've had it up to here with you." Her hand sliced the air above her head to give him a better idea of her frustration level.

"Bren," Fletch said quietly, catching her hand in his. "I need you."

She really should pull her fingers from his grip, she thought, but she left them where they were.

"I admit I'm scum," Fletch said.

"The lowest," she agreed.

"A flake."

"Mmm."

"A creep."

Bren had no argument to offer on that one, either.

"But you are my oldest and best friend," Fletch continued. "A good friend."

"I'm resigning from the position. The responsibility is too great." Bren tried to slip her hand free of his. Perversely, Fletch held on.

Damn him! she thought, and felt tears begin to well in her eyes. Damn him, damn him, damn him.

There was no way she was going to let him see this further evidence that she was female. A state she could do nothing to correct, even though he seemed blind to the fact.

Gathering pride like a mantle around her, Bren blinked back the tears and lifted her chin at a determined angle. "You've got four days left to make your decision, Layton," she growled. "And you can damn well do it on your own."

Amazed at her vehemence, Fletch watched her speechlessly. This was the woman her male co-workers despaired of ever impressing, the same males who pitied him, thinking she found him even more invisible than they were. But he wasn't. The fact that her lovely green eyes glittered with something more than anger proved it. Too late he realized the sparkles were tears.

Oh, hell.

"All right," Fletch agreed softly, "I'll do it on my own."

He'd thought there was no way her eyes could look more lovely than they had the night before, but now, as they registered drenched surprise, Fletch recognized that he'd been wrong. With strong emotion Bren's eyes deepened until they were the shade of high-quality emeralds.

"You—you mean that?" she stuttered.

Fletch drew her hand to his shirtfront, moving it so that her fingers traced a design over his chest. "Cross my heart," he promised. "I'm sorry I made you cry, Bren."

Her hand fluttered against him, feeling as fragile as the butterfly he'd once caught in his cupped hands when he was a boy.

"Yeah, right," Bren said, her voice gruff with suppressed emotion. "You've already made it clear that girl stuff like that is out of character for me."

Fletch sighed deeply. "I'm an idiot, all right?" At least he wasn't alone in being one if Mick, Kurt and Steve were to be believed. "I opened my mouth before I thought," he said.

"You should know better," Bren mumbled. She tried once more to disentangle her fingers from his, but Fletch wasn't about to let her go yet.

"Forgive me?" he asked.

She shrugged, her eyes not meeting his.

"Friends again?" he persisted.

"I suppose." She didn't sound sure, Fletch noted. Not a good sign.

"Brenda?" he murmured quietly.

At his use of her formal name, her eyes flew to his. Her lips parted in surprise.

Fletch followed his gut instinct. His free hand brushed along her jawline, his fingers tilting her chin up. Before he could think better of the action, his lips brushed lightly over hers.

He'd only meant to soothe her. Hadn't he? But the bolt of desire that zapped through his system had each and every one of his senses immediately attuned to Bren's scent, taste and softness. Without bothering to think about what he was doing, Fletch kissed her again, taking the time to savor the exotic sensation of having her mouth slightly open and complacent beneath his.

It was only when Bren gasped that his brain kicked back into gear and Fletch wondered if he'd made a big mistake.

It hadn't felt like a mistake. It had felt right. Good. Better than good.

Snatching her hand from his grip, Bren glared up at him. "Don't you dare think that, just because I occasionally display a few feminine traits, you can treat me like one of those brainless twerps you collect," she snarled under her breath.

Fletch wouldn't have blamed her if she hauled off and slugged him.

Rather than defend himself, he kept quiet. At the rate he was going, he'd be chewing shoe leather if he dared open his mouth.

"Damn you!" Bren rammed her fist into his arm again. She was losing steam, though. Earlier on the plane, she'd hit him harder. "Why'd you have to do that?"

"I wanted to," Fletch confessed. To do so seemed safer than prevarication at the moment.

"You should have warned me first," Bren said.

"Next time, I will," he promised. "Friends again?"

"Friends," she agreed.

"Prove it," Fletch dared her. "Challenge me to a game of Commandos in Space."

Bren smiled faintly. "How will that prove we're friends? I'll beat you at it. I'm the undisputed champ at Home-run Harry's."

"I've been practicing," Fletch said. "I'll even supply the quarters."

She hesitated for two loud beats of his heart, then held out her hand. "Deal."

Rather than shake hands, which somehow smacked of the despised eunuch treatment, Fletch wove his fingers with hers and tugged Bren toward the airport game room. "How does this sound?" he asked. "If you win, you don't have to play shrink with me over Dominique anymore. If I win, I won't plague you with what I should do over her ultimatum."

"You're letting me off the hook? Totally off the hook?" Bren demanded, clearly in awe of the idea.

"Well, this particular hook," Fletch agreed. "I hope that you'll be willing to help me out the next time I get in a spot."

"You do tend to get into tight corners," she said.

Fletch smiled in relief. His Bren was back. "Listen," he said, "if you ever find yourself with a problem or in trouble or—"

"I'll call you," she promised with a smile.

Mick, Kurt and Steve were right, Fletch thought. Her grins were casual, impish and downright devastating. The twenty-four-thousand-dollar question was why had it taken him so long to notice?

5

Day four: Wednesday
> The adage that all is fair in love and war is particularly true at this stage in your campaign, so pull out all the stops. Choose clothing that leaves him in no doubt that you are a woman. Do continue to keep him confused. While you want him very aware of you, act as if you are not as aware of him.
>
> *Land Your Man*

Jet lag and three time-zone changes made the idea of starting work on the Bailey and Salazar trade-show booth any earlier than noon ridiculous. At least as far as Fletch was concerned. And, considering he was in charge of this expedition, the rest of the team was willing to go along with his decision.

Even Bren.

Fletch figured she was too tired, both emotionally and physically, to argue with him. Although she'd whipped him at all three video games they'd played, the shadow of distrust remained in her eyes. He'd

hoped to chase it away by teaching her to play pin-
ball, one of the few games Bren had never attempted
before. Positioned behind her, her body nearly
spooned with his, his hands covering hers on the pad-
dle buttons, Fletch had been pretty sure he could turn
her mood around. A few quick jabs of her elbow in his
rib cage had discouraged that bit of male arrogance,
though.

He counted himself lucky to emerge from the forced
layover with only a few bruises, most of them suf-
fered by his ego. There had been a moment or two
worth remembering—like the contentment he'd felt
when they stood silently side by side at the floor-to-
ceiling gate window and watched the rain soak the already swimming runways. Or the fact that she still allowed him to drop a companionable arm around her
shoulders as they strolled the length of the concourse.
The way she turned naturally into his arms when they
were airborne once more and then fell asleep. That all-
too-brief kiss.

He thought a lot about the kiss.

About Bren's confession that she had been in love.

And about what Mick, Kurt and Steve had said
about her effect on them.

All in all, it had been a fairly sleepless night, made
worse by the fact that there was a connecting door between his room and Bren's. One that was, at his own
request, not locked.

It was still unlocked, but he hadn't tried the door
until he heard her leave her room that morning. The
look in her eyes the evening before had been encouraging only to a man eager for castration, which he

wasn't. Hopefully, his luck would improve by the coming evening. Up to this point he'd been playing at seducing Bren, but now he was serious. He had a definite plan in mind and enough determination to pull it off in record time. He had a deadline. Not the one of Dominique's creation, but of his own.

By Saturday, when the trade show ended, he wanted Bren to have fallen in love with him.

Because, during his long, sleepless night, he'd come to the conclusion that he was, and had always been, in love with her. No wonder he had flinched away from committing himself to spending his life with Dominique. He had already spent most of his life with Bren, and had enjoyed every moment of it, too. Why break a winning streak?

At the moment, of course, it didn't feel much like a winning streak. All it took to turn that around was to switch on the charm. Once Bren started succumbing, well, then he'd decide what came next. First he had to get her undivided attention, keep her off-balance. A cinch for an experienced player like himself, Fletch assured his reflection as he pushed through the glass doors and into the echoing, air-conditioned cavern of the city convention center.

Bren's greeting was far from encouraging when he reached the area allocated for the B and S booth. She gave him a slow and rather insulting perusal, her glittering eyes sweeping from his casually styled hair to his white polo shirt, sharply creased khaki trousers and highly buffed loafers. "Don't feel like working, Mr. Layton?" she asked dryly.

Fletch took in her own running shoes, jeans, form-engulfing T-shirt and rumpled curls, then the similar outfits worn by Mick, Kurt and Steve. The booth area looked like a giant child's playground, with large shipping boxes piled in a haphazard manner as if they were blocks. Bright orange extension cords criss-crossed the concrete floor, attached to hand-held tools, a bank of lights and a box fan. A jungle-gym affair of plumbing pipes was in the process of being erected, the spare parts still scattered around. Both Mick and Steve had mounted stepladders, and the muscle-bound Kurt was actually wearing a tool belt.

"Okay, so I dressed wrong," Fletch admitted. "Tell me what you want done, and I'll do it."

There was a long, yellow pencil stuck behind Bren's ear. She plucked it free and picked up a clipboard from atop a nearby box. "Hmm." She chewed lightly on the pencil as she flipped through various sheets of paper, considering items on her incessant lists.

As if mesmerized, Fletch stared at the way her teeth clamped around the pencil. They were dainty, gleaming white, straight teeth. The perfect choppers for advertising toothpaste. They hadn't always been, though. Hadn't she had a crooked canine as a kid? Fletch cast his mind back, trying to remember, and came up with a picture of an impish, metal-banded grin instead. Braces!

No one would guess Mother Nature had mis-formed Bren's bite, not the way those pearly whites sank—rather erotically, he thought—into the wood of her pencil. When Fletch looked away, he found the other three men as entranced with Bren's gritted ivories as he had been.

She glanced up, reclaimed the pencil to make a note on one of her sheets, then slipped the pencil back into her chestnut curls. "There isn't much to be done that will keep you clean," she reported. "I'd send you back to the hotel to change, but chances are we'd never see you again."

"So don't send me," Fletch suggested, pulling himself free from an image of nibbling on that unseen ear. "If I'm not worried about my clothes, you shouldn't be."

"Yes, I should," Bren countered. "Mom gave you that shirt last Christmas. If you ruin it, and she finds out I let you, she'll kill me."

"Easily taken care of," Fletch said. And an excellent opportunity to make an impression on her. He stripped the pristine shirt over his head and tossed it aside, flexing his nicely defined muscles a bit, as if loosening them up.

Bren didn't bat an eye at the display, but Mick, Kurt and Steve shot him deadly looks. So he wasn't playing fair. So what? They were welcome to shed their shirts as well. If they did, the only physique that would best his was Kurt's, and she'd already shot the advertising man down in the past.

"What do you want me to do first?" Fletch asked, his teeth glinting in a cocksure grin.

"Put your shirt back on," Bren said.

His grin went limp. She'd barely glanced at him. Hadn't given one sign that she found his pecs distracting. No sighs or languishing looks. Not even an admiring one.

Okay, so maybe it had been an adolescent ploy, but it had always worked nicely for him in the past, with other women.

The women Bren termed brainless twerps.

Maybe that was why taking his shirt off had worked with them. Bren, of course, was different. Worthy of his best effort.

Besides, it was still early in this ball game. The batter was still at the plate with only a single strike against him. He was far from being struck out yet.

"Why don't you go find a phone, Fletch, and order the rest of us some lunch," Bren said. "While you're gone, I'll find the box with the Fresh All Day giveaway T-shirts. That way you can change into one when you get back."

Mick, Kurt and Steve exchanged satisfied grins and went back to work as Fletch tugged his shirt back over his head. He could almost hear them thinking *eunuch* again. He gritted his teeth in a not-so-pleasant grimace. Bren had her back to him so she didn't see the challenge he issued via a glare to the other men.

"Right," Fletch said. He'd show them who the eunuchs were. Via lunch. "I'd ask what you want to eat, but whaddya say I surprise you instead?"

All it took was Bren's smile of agreement and he was gone, a hastily concocted plan hatching as he went.

Fletch had been out of sight all of two seconds when Bren felt someone at her shoulder. She looked up in surprise to find her three co-workers regarding her with long, serious faces.

"Uh, Bren? Could we talk to you?" Kurt asked.

"Sure." Bren put down her clipboard. "What's up?"

"Layton," Mick mumbled under his breath.

"We just thought you should be warned about your friend there," Steve said, jerking his chin in the direction Fletch had disappeared.

"Warned? About what?" she demanded.

"You're a challenge to him," Kurt said.

"He's the only guy you ever let get close to you," Mick added.

"And he's set to take advantage of that," Steve muttered, still frowning.

Bren stared at them in surprise. A moment later, she grinned widely. "Tell me another one," she urged.

When they didn't smile back at her, Bren's eyes grew wide. "You're serious!"

"Damn right we are," Steve insisted.

"We made a mistake," Mick said.

"A big one in talking to Layton about you," Kurt agreed. "We thought he was one of us."

"Sort of," Mick added. "Oh, we knew you were old friends, but we thought that if he was interested in you, he would have made his move long ago."

"Besides, you didn't seem to be his type, considering he hangs out with that beauty queen," Kurt said.

"Not that we don't think you aren't beauty queen material, too," Steve amended quickly. "Actually, you're worth a couple of Dominiques."

"A good dozen of 'em," Mick said.

Bren rubbed the center of her forehead, attempting to massage away the hint of a headache that suddenly threatened. "What do you mean, Fletch is interested in me?"

The men exchanged uneasy glances. "Well, you know. Uh, as a woman," Kurt mumbled, his neck turning bright red with embarrassment.

"As a woman?" Bren repeated.

"We figure he only got the idea after we told him you were sorta blind to the way we all feel about you," Steve said.

"The way you feel about me?" Bren sank back to rest against a rung of the nearest stepladder. "What are you talking about? We're all pals. I'm everybody's kid sister. The team shortstop. And I've got to tell you, guys, I really appreciate the way you all treat me like an equal around the office *and* on the softball team."

Mick looked toward the roofing girders far above them. "Did we bring any rope along? That one looks strong enough to hang myself on."

Bren punched him softly on the arm. "Don't talk like that. So you all talked to Fletch about me. I'm the only female on this trip. It's natural for you to mention me."

"We didn't just mention you. You were the only topic of conversation," Steve confessed quickly. "And what we all said was that we don't think of you as our kid sister, buddy or pal. None of the men in the office do, Bren."

"Don't be ridiculous," Bren insisted. "I know the way you all treat me, guys."

"No, it's the way you treat us," Kurt said. "Like we're your equal."

Bren shook her head, sure she wasn't hearing right.

"You don't male bash like the other women do," Mick explained.

She smiled at that. "You haven't heard me talk about Fletch or my brother, have you."

"As far as we're concerned, they might deserve your scorn," Steve said.

"Layton sure does," Kurt muttered darkly.

"But more important, Bren, you never notice when a guy is physically attracted to you," Mick said.

She laughed out loud at that. "Attracted to me? You're kidding. I'm not the kind of girl guys drool over."

Their combined expressions told her she was dead wrong using that argument.

My God! Sally was right! The book did work—too well!

What have I done? Bren moaned silently. She'd been a skeptic, had not realized the advice in *Land Your Man* was as lethal as a loaded gun. And, rather than being careful in using the strategies, she'd been flaunting them, unaware that they possessed a hair trigger.

"You're kidding!" Bren insisted, flabbergasted. "Then why hasn't anyone at B and S ever asked me out?"

"I tried," Kurt said. "You didn't even know that's what I was doing."

"Oh, I'm sorry," she murmured, lightly touching his shoulder. "Forgive me?"

Kurt brightened. "So you will go out with me?"

"Well, actually..." Bren looked away so she wouldn't have to see the disappointment in his face. "It isn't as if I don't like you, Kurt," she hastened to add, "but do you know Meg in accounting? If I went out with you, she'd never speak to me again. I shouldn't be telling you this, so promise you won't tell. She's got a crush on you."

Steve clapped Kurt on the shoulder. "Which is akin to having one man on base already," he said.

"Maybe I should give her a call, huh?" Kurt asked.

"And while he's calling her, you can have dinner with me, Bren," Mick suggested.

Bren shook her head slowly. "Jill in customer service," she murmured.

"She told me she never wanted to see me again," Mick said.

"She lied." Bren turned to Steve before he could add an invitation of his own. "Meredith only started seeing Vince because she wanted to make you jealous," she told him.

"I knew that," he insisted, but he was a terrible liar. "How did you know, though?"

"Company grapevine," Bren admitted. "News on it has been pretty dull lately, but once you three get home it should perk up quite a bit."

Mick shoved his hands into his jeans pockets. "You're a good friend, Bren. Sorry we screwed things up for you so royally."

"Yeah," Kurt agreed. "If you want, we could catch Layton in a dark alley and break his kneecaps or something."

"No way, guys. He's the best base stealer on our softball team. If we want to be in the championship play-offs, Fletch needs to stay healthy," she reminded them.

Steve sighed. "Then what about after the season is over?" he suggested.

"Maybe," Bren said. "For now, leave him to me."

Mick chuckled. "You know, guys, the way she said that, I almost pity Layton."

Bren made sure she dug out a Fresh All Day T-shirt before Fletch returned. An extra-large one so it wouldn't conform to that spectacular chest.

She really shouldn't have felt breathless at the sight of it. She'd seen that same chest bare through all its stages of development. It was just this particular stage that made her own chest feel tight, her lungs constricted.

When her fingers stroked over the T-shirt he'd soon be donning, Bren hoped that, if the men behind her noticed the action, they'd think she was simply smoothing wrinkles from the fabric. Her mind was deep in fantasyland, though, imagining what it would feel like to slip her fingertips through the entrancing dark hair on Fletch's chest. To cuddle up to him. To kiss him again.

Even if he was a creep.

Which he most definitely was if what Mick, Kurt and Steve had said was true.

It had an awfully clear ring of truth about it. Which was depressing. However, considering Fletch had never treated her as a desirable woman in the past, the fact that he was making an effort to be charming to her now was suspicious. And mean.

Didn't he realize that she was a person? That it would be so easy to give in to her love for him? That the hurt when he rejected or forgot about her would be crippling because she did care so much for him?

Of course, he didn't realize any of that. He was a man. A pigheaded, selfish, egotistical, blind, incredibly handsome, sweet, tender, loving man. Damn. She couldn't even malign him decently. He'd always been her knight in shining armor. Her ideal. Her friend.

That didn't mean she intended to be kind in teaching him a lesson.

Bren pawed through the other boxes, found what she wanted and hastily slipped the bag deep into the trash container. She waited until Fletch returned to begin her performance.

"Rats," she hissed, just loudly enough for all four of the men to hear. "How could shipping have neglected to put pencils in with the other supplies? I know I sent them down."

"Pencils?" Fletch asked.

Bren saw him looking at the one she had stuck behind her ear. She reclaimed it and chewed thoughtfully on the shaft. It was rewarding to see his eyes drop to her lips. Obviously all those hours spent jealously watching his old girlfriends had paid off, Bren mused. In a way, it had been seduction school. And if that was what it took to teach him a lesson, she was going to pull every one of the tricks she'd observed and augment them with *Land Your Man*'s strategies.

Mentally she went over the list of things she'd once thought too silly to use and chose one. She'd bone up on others later.

"Yeah, pencils," Bren said, and threw in a giant sigh of disappointment. Her chest swelled with the movement.

Behind Fletch, Kurt's mouth dropped open. Steve pushed it shut for him and winked at Mick.

More stoic than his compatriots, Fletch kept his gaze glued to her face, although there was a hint of strain in his eyes at the effort, Bren was pleased to note.

"You know," she said, tossing in a moue of pique for good measure. "Those little short ones like they have at the miniature golf course."

"Short ones," Fletch repeated.

"Like this," Bren insisted, and poised thumb and forefinger to illustrate four inches. "Although they might be longer."

She was pleased when he had to clear his throat before answering. His mind had obviously conjured up a situation far removed from the need for pencils. Just as she'd hoped it would.

How convenient it was to know a man's peccadilloes so well, Bren thought with pleasure.

"Do we really need them?" Fletch asked.

"Need them? Quite desperately, really," she said. "How else are visitors going to fill out their entry blanks for the grand prize?"

"Grand prize?"

She shook her head sadly. "You never do read the promotional materials one minute before you have to, do you? Show him the poster, Mick."

Mick looked happy to oblige and snapped the rolled sheet so that it uncurled over the packing boxes.

"The winner gets to enjoy a cruise in the Bahamas," Bren said, gliding her fingertips over the ad, supposedly to hold it in place. "Five days of balmy breezes, warm sun and four long, sultry nights. The drawing will be done before the trade show ends this weekend."

"Oh," Fletch murmured. "I guess we do need pencils then."

Bren tossed him the logo-decorated T-shirt. "If you help the guys set everything up, I'll run out and find an office-supply store where I can buy some. Uh, it might take me a while since I'm not familiar with the town. Is that all right?"

"Fine with us," Kurt said.

"Don't worry. We can handle it," Mick agreed.

"Hey, what should we do with your lunch when it arrives?" Steve asked.

"Eat it," Bren recommended.

"But it's your favorite," Fletch sputtered.

"Oh, how sweet," Bren cooed. "But I'll have to pass on lunch for now. I'll grab something while I'm out. That sound okay to you, Fletch?"

He shrugged and tried to cover the fact that she'd just cut the ground out from under him. *Good try, pal,* Bren thought, pleased with herself.

"Hey," Fletch said, "we need pencils. What else can we do?"

She scooped up her tote-bag purse and the trash wherein she'd hidden the pencils. "I'll drop this off on my way out," she said. "See you later."

Before she tossed the trash bag in the Dumpster, she retrieved the stubby pencils and quickly slipped them into her jumbo purse. It took only a few minutes to whistle up a taxi. "Where's the closest mall?" Bren asked the driver as she slipped into the rear seat.

"Depends on what kind of store you want, lady. You got Sears and Penneys at the Boulevard or Saks at the Fashion Show."

Bren leaned back into the seat cushions, very satisfied with the way things were going. "Oh, in that case, make it the Fashion Show by all means," she drawled lazily. "And step on it."

Fletch leaned against the tiles and let the shower pulse water on his back. Since he'd barely touched the hot tap, it was rather icy water.

It didn't cure the way he felt. It didn't even help.

He was obviously losing his touch. Every nuance of his plan to turn Bren on had backfired on him—a hundredfold, if the racing of his blood was anything to go on.

To prove he could be diligent on the job, he'd done far more manual labor that afternoon than he had over the last six years. Every muscle in his back had bent to her beck and call—and was complaining loudly as a result. Had Bren noticed? No, she'd taken all his efforts for granted and hadn't even given him a thank-you-very-much-for-getting-blisters look.

But she'd given Kurt an awfully sincere smile, patted Mick on the back—literally—and tossed Steve a blatant come-on line in regards to dinner. Fortunately, the lethally seasoned lunch Fletch had ordered had felled his immediate competition as per plan. All three men had bowed out of enjoying evening entertainments and retired to their rooms to nurse bottles of antacid.

Now if only his own effusive compliments hadn't ricocheted off Bren's force field, Fletch would be rolling in clover. Or preferably, among downy hotel bed sheets. But such was not the case. Bren had been deaf to his words.

And considering that Mick, Kurt and Steve had gone to such pains yesterday to tell him how casually Bren treated them, she had been damn flirty with each of them when she returned to the convention center three hours after leaving it.

Las Vegas, apparently, had so little need for stubby pencils that it had taken her that long to find a supply of them. Considering the city was ringed with golf courses, Fletch found that hard to believe and wondered what else Bren had done besides make a stop at the hotel to pick up a change of clothing for him. And to re-create herself.

He still had a hard time recognizing little Brenda Burton in the siren who'd spent the afternoon treating him exactly as the other men had pointed out she did. Like a harmless eunuch.

Fletch leaned into the jet of cold water, praying it would work magic on his extremely healthy libido.

Knowing it wouldn't. Not with Bren looking the way she had that afternoon.

She had still been dressed in jeans and running shoes when she returned, but the all-concealing, oversize T-shirt had been replaced with a body-hugging white tank top that set off her light tan and enhanced the supple grace of her bare arms and the elegant line of her very visible collarbone. Since the fit of her jeans was now on display as well, having Bren bend over one of the packing boxes had been so distracting he'd dropped the screwdriver he'd been using and nearly brained Steve, who, fortunately, hadn't noticed Bren's action. Kurt had ended up chewing on his fist in frustration.

The worst had been when Fletch realized that from atop the ladder, it was possible to get an even more enticing view of Bren's charms via her low-cut neckline. Particularly when she stood at the base of the ladder and looked up at the man working on the booth design above her. Mick had called her over for consultations quite often. And she'd given him long, languid looks with those gorgeous green eyes of hers at every conference.

Fletch ground his teeth at the memory.

Well, there weren't going to be any other staffers around this evening to put a stick in his spokes. And to make sure Bren understood just how bad a state he was in over her, Fletch decided, he was going to ooze charm. Use everything he knew about her tastes, her likes, her dislikes, to land her right where she belonged. In his arms.

In his bed.

If he still had the energy left to even get her there, that is. To make sure he woke up sufficiently, Fletch turned off the hot water completely. A rain of icelike water pelted his chest. Considering the way he was feeling about Bren, Fletch was a bit surprised it didn't turn to steam the moment it hit him.

Bren stared closely at Fletch. He was dressed much as he had been earlier in the day, only his slacks were dove gray and his shirt a deep charcoal. He looked handsome and yet strange.

"How come your lips are blue?" she asked.

"Had the air-conditioning turned up too high," he explained—rather glibly, she thought—and slipped his arm around her waist. "You're welcome to warm them up."

Bren allowed herself the pleasure of being pressed close to his chest for the space of one breath before eluding him. "Oh, I'm sure once you start talking all that hot air will have them defrosted in no time," she assured him. "Do you think I look okay for a night on the town here?" She already knew the answer, having been gushed over not only by the Saks sales associate but by two shoppers who were passing when she left the dressing room.

For good measure though, Bren extended her arms and twirled slightly, so that the full, short skirt of her flowered, black-and-white halter dress flared out. As she'd intended, Fletch's eyes dropped to her legs, then cruised slowly back to her face.

"You look beautiful, Bren," he said seriously. "You always look beautiful to me."

"Well, you always look handsome to me, too," she said, making sure her voice was light and teasing rather than serious.

Thank goodness she'd stuck *Land Your Man* in her suitcase. She'd studied it while soaking in a very tepid bath; considering the sizzling looks Fletch had been giving her all afternoon, hot water hadn't appealed to her at all.

She was already in hot water by being so hopelessly in love with him. And so out of her natural sphere in flirting outrageously with every man in sight. Talk about draining a woman's strength!

The book had been a big help and now, with a couple of chapters under her belt—a wide, waist-defining belt the book claimed men liked—Bren felt confident, secure and powerfully feminine.

To test her new power, she gave Fletch a slow once-over. Although she'd been expecting a response, it wasn't the hot flare that sparked to life in his eyes. Or the answering warmth that look conjured in the vicinity of her rib cage.

Well, what woman wouldn't respond to that determined, smoky gaze? His already dark hazel eyes seemed to grow denser, deeper. His lazy grin, when coupled with the faint, sexy cleft in his chin, was deadly enough to begin with.

Bren danced away from him, countering the magnetic force that seemed to pull her closer to him. "Now, didn't you promise me a birthday dinner and a glimpse of the nightlife as a present?" she asked.

"Absolutely, sweetheart," Fletch agreed. His grin turned from lazy to raffish. His hand slid sensuously over her bared back.

Chills of awareness skittered up Bren's spine.

"I really like this dress," Fletch said. "Did you get it especially for this trip?"

"Oh, this? I've had it for a while," Bren said. A while being nearly three hours. The only outfits she'd packed had been blouses and comfortably pleated trousers. Not exactly items for a seduction trousseau.

"Well, you look spectacular in it," Fletch murmured. "So much so, it's tempting to just stay in and not share you with anyone."

Bren shook her head, letting her curls tumble in abandon. "Not a good idea, slick. I checked the TV schedule, and there is nada on the tube. Besides, how often do I get to a place like Las Vegas? It's my birthday and I want to play tonight."

"Then we'll play," Fletch announced, giving her a slight shove toward the door. "First stop is dinner and a jousting match at the Excalibur. From there, we'll work our way back up the Strip, doing whatever you wish, my lady."

Bren stomped down on an unhappy sigh. Although the itinerary sounded like fun, she wished they weren't playacting. That he actually was in love with her. Wanted her.

Well, perhaps he did want her. A little bit. She doubted the desire she'd read in his eyes was totally manufactured. Even Fletch couldn't pretend to that degree.

Could he?

* * *

It was going to kill him, Fletch decided. Every sense shouted that he should yank her into his arms, kiss her silly and then move on to even more pleasurable events. With any other women, it was exactly the play he would have made. But this was Bren.

Bren, who meant more to him than getting to first base or driving in a satisfying home run, which was pretty much the context in which he'd viewed all his previous romantic liaisons. With other women he would have arranged a quiet, intimate dinner in a dark, expensive restaurant. He would have let them revel in candlelight, white linen and strolling violinists, then would have stepped up to bat. In fact, his first instinct had been to find just such a place. His second had been to ferret out the kind of place Bren would appreciate far more. Eating with her fingers while watching guys in tights take dramatic swings at each other with swords fit the bill. Tomorrow night would be even better. The local minor-league baseball team would be playing on their home field, and he already had two tickets for the game in his pocket.

And, Fletch admitted to himself, his planned scenarios sounded like a lot more fun to him than the pricy romantic dinners of his rakish past. With Bren he could be himself, not a Lothario.

Which was probably why it had taken him so long to realize the woman he wanted had been under his nose all his life. He'd always separated his love life from his real life in the past. Blending them now had a real appeal—but only if he could have Bren at his side.

"You know, I feel really guilty," she said when they were in a taxi and stuck in Strip traffic. "I promised you I'd help you make up your mind about Dominique and then I ducked out on you. You've only got three days before the deadline, Fletch. Have you made a decision yet?"

He wasn't going to let the shadow of Dominique intrude on what boded to be the perfect evening. He twisted in his seat to gawk at the passing scene. "Hey, is that the Mirage's volcano?" he asked the cabdriver.

"Yep, that's it. Looks more impressive after dark," the man said.

"Looks kind of pretty now as a waterfall," Fletch said. "What say we take it in later, Bren?"

He was pleased when she craned in her seat to look back. "That's a volcano?"

"Man-made, of course. I understand it metamorphoses on a regular schedule."

"Las Vegas's answer to Old Faithful?"

"Something like that," Fletch agreed. He slipped his arm around her bare shoulders. "You sure you aren't going to catch cold in this getup? The hotels have all got the air-conditioning really cranked up."

"If I want to warm up, all I have to do is take one step outside and be in the blast furnace again," Bren assured him. "You know, I heard that dry heat didn't feel as bad as the humid heat we have back home, but now that I've felt it, I don't see much difference."

"Hot is hot," the cabdriver interjected, "especially once you top 110 degrees. Where you folks from?"

Fletch let Bren carry the conversation. She'd always been a good people person, honestly interested in whatever they had to tell her. She made them feel good just to be in her company. He swelled with pride for her as the cabdriver reeled out a story about moving his family to Vegas after one visit.

"Wife loves the heat," he said, wrapping up the tale as they stopped before the lofty, castlelike facade of the Excalibur Hotel. "Good luck at the tables," he added as Fletch waved off his offer of change for a twenty, thereby passing along a generous tip.

Bren stared up at the brightly roofed towers that rose above them, her lips parted enticingly with the motion. Fletch decided to take her unconscious invitation and dropped a light, teasing kiss on her lips before sweeping her forward into the hotel.

"What was that for?" Bren asked, grinning up at him in surprise.

"Just testing to see if you were using Fresh All Day toothpaste," Fletch said.

Bren came to an abrupt halt. "I don't believe it!" she gasped. "You actually got the product name right!"

He chuckled softly. "Hey, you knew I'd get it in the long run," he teased. "But, you know, that taste test was far too short to satisfy me. Let's try it again."

Fletch was relieved when she grinned happily at the suggestion. When he kissed her the second time, Bren kissed him back.

If he'd ever fantasized about kissing her in the past, Fletch doubted he could have dreamed up a more ego-building experience. Or a more erotically promising one.

Her lips clung to his, caressed them softly. He savored the sensation, content to have time come to a complete standstill. She seemed as reluctant to end the caress as he was.

Which showed she wasn't as immune to him as she tried make him think, Fletch mused happily.

"Mmm," he murmured when Bren broke the kiss. "Based on how delightful you taste, we should sell a ton of toothpaste."

"Hope so," Bren said. She slipped her arm companionably around his waist, all her previous artifice gone. She might not be dressed like the old Bren, but she was back to being the friend he'd known forever. The girl who'd been his best friend for nearly twenty years.

The one he was now picturing in a satin-sheeted bed rather than on a dusty baseball diamond.

"I'm really proud of you," Fletch said, guiding her through the casino crowd. "You've got a terrific promotion going."

Bren rolled her eyes. "It isn't like I was the creative force at work here, slick. I'm one of the little people."

"Little but mighty," he countered. "Don't try to tell me Fresh All Day isn't your pet project. I've seen the way you've leapt to its defense time and again over the last few months."

"It's my job."

"Like hell," Fletch said. "It's your baby. Advertising will miss you when you leave."

She leaned back. Fortunately, into the crook of his arm. "Who says I'm leaving?"

"You will," he murmured. "Word gets out. You'll get an offer too good to ignore and—"

"Yeah, right."

"Could happen."

"And I could get abducted by little green men from Mars," Bren said. "What are you doing—sounding me out as a future member of top management?"

"Just pointing out that you have options, sweetheart. I'm not really part of your department, remember? I'm just on loan from sales for the trade show."

"Oh, really. That doesn't answer my question, Fletch."

"Okay. How's this sound? Even if you confessed that you detested every moment on the job, word of your discontent would not originate with me. I belong to you first and B and S second."

There was a line of guests waiting to enter the medieval banqueting hall. Fletch and Bren merged into it. Dominique would have balked at anything that involved standing in line, Fletch mused silently. She would have sneered at the evening's entertainment, finding it beneath her.

Dominique didn't have the least idea of how to have fun.

Bren, on the other hand...

She chuckled. "You belong to me first?" she echoed. "Aren't you forgetting Dominique in this lineup?"

Not one bit. By comparing Bren to her he was only beginning to discover what a close call he'd had.

Fletch put a finger beneath Bren's chin and tilted it, ensuring that her eyes would meet his. "I mean what I say, Bren," he told her.

"I know better. You're in sales, Fletch."

"Not where you're concerned. I love you, Bren."

Her smile quivered slightly before holding steady. "Yeah, I know, slick," she said.

Which meant she didn't believe one word. Not the way he'd meant it. It was a good thing the night was still young. His silver tongue was going to have to do one hell of a sales job.

Damned if he wasn't looking forward to every word it took, too.

She couldn't have asked for a more perfect evening, Bren mused as they strolled back into their hotel. From the rollicking dinner, where knights tilted as the crowd cheered them on, she and Fletch had walked hand in hand up Las Vegas Boulevard, the Strip, to Caesar's Palace. The classical statues were quite a change from the medieval trappings they'd just left, but the noise of the casino remained the same. Bren was pleased when Fletch showed no interest in dropping coins in any of the machines or joining a game at one of the blackjack or craps tables. It meant she had him all to herself rather than sharing him with Lady Luck.

He knew all her weaknesses and tugged her aboard Cleopatra's barge for a drink—a tequila sunrise complete with fruit. While he sipped his Scotch, the content expression on his face told her that he was enjoying their time together as much as she was. Rather than ruin the moment, Bren bit her tongue to keep from bringing Dominique's name up again. Perhaps procrastination was catching, she thought, but putting off getting Fletch to make a decision about the beautiful bimbo seemed like an awfully good idea.

Some things couldn't be pushed off, though, so after window-shopping at the Forum and enjoying the volcano's eruption, Bren reminded Fletch that they had an early morning at the trade show. He didn't even argue with her, but flagged a cab.

The casino at their hotel was hopping as well, but when they boarded the elevator, Fletch and Bren were the only passengers. For two floors they stood apart, not even holding hands as they had most of the evening. Of course, Bren reminded herself, they had done so simply to avoid being separated in the crowds. That didn't mean she couldn't miss his closeness now. Or turn off her awareness of him.

"Bren?" Fletch said quietly, as he stepped closer to her.

She turned slightly, looking up at him. "Mmm?"

Another floor went by as he gazed silently into her eyes. He lifted a hand to her hair.

It probably looked a wreck, tumbled by a pleasant desert breeze earlier.

Fletch's fingers slid into the mass of curls and cupped the nape of her neck, drawing her into a kiss that was nothing like the ones he'd given her before. This was the kind she'd dreamed of receiving, of sharing, of returning. It was tender, demanding and hot. Oh, so hot.

Bren gave herself up to the sweetness of it, welcoming the slant of his mouth over hers, and a sigh later, the entrance of his tongue between her lips.

When their floor was reached and the doors slid open, Fletch didn't seem to notice. He deepened the caress, his hands moving down her bare back, molding her closer to him, then back up to fumble with the halter fastening of her dress.

Bren broke away, blinking at him in shock. Good God! What was she doing? It was one thing to dream about giving herself to him, but quite another to actually do so. Especially since she knew he was only interested in another conquest, not a relationship. At least not with her. Dominique's carefully made-up face gloated in Bren's mind.

"Whoa!" she exclaimed. "We're here already." Knowing it looked like she was escaping, she dashed off the elevator and down the hall toward her room.

"Bren!" Fletch called, his long legs eating up the distance she was trying so desperately to put between them. She was at her door, digging in her purse for the card key, when he gripped her upper arms and forced her to look at him. "Wait a minute. We've got to—"

"Apologize big-time," she interrupted. "Blame it on the sunrise. Much as I love tequila cocktails, I don't have them very often. Guess I forgot who I was with."

Fletch shook her slightly. "Stop it. You weren't the one who started it and I knew exactly who I was with, Bren."

Her eyes fell from his. "Then I wish you'd stop pretending I'm one of your flirts and leave me alone."

His hands dropped away from her. "You don't mean that."

Bren shoved the key in the door and darted past him into her room. Fletch followed, pausing only long enough to lock the door behind him.

"Steve and the others told me what you're up to, Fletch," Bren said. "I've become a challenge, and who knows better than I do that you can't resist picking up gauntlets when they are thrown?"

"That isn't what this is," he said.

"Isn't it?" She spun away from him, tossing her purse on the bed. "Well, it was a challenge for me. After all, I'm as bad as you are in resisting them. Can't let one rest." Bren raised a hand to her brow, fingertips grazing the small white crescent near her right eye. "I've even got the scars to prove it," she added bitterly.

Fletch sighed deeply. "So this has all been a game, is that it?"

"Exactly that. I've always wondered what it would be like to be Dominique, and since she's the kind of woman you obviously prefer, I used her as my role model," Bren said. She kept her back to him, afraid that if she faced him he'd see the hurt she needed so much to disguise. "Worked pretty well, huh? But, as you should know, I'm not anything like Dominique and it hasn't been that much fun being her, after all. Think I'll just go back to being plain old Bren again."

"You've never been plain or—"

She whirled on him. "Compliments? Oh, back off, Fletch. Save it for Dominique."

Since neither of them had bothered to turn on the lights, she could barely see his expression in the starlit room. His stance was stiff, as if he was affronted by her attack. Him! The guy who'd started it all to begin with.

"It's time you shaped up. You'll probably be married on Monday," she said accusingly.

"I hope so," he said quietly.

He was dead serious.

Bren's heart broke directly in half. "So, you have made your decision."

"Yes."

It took a Herculean effort to hold back the pain, but she did it. "Congratulations, Fletch. I hope you'll be very happy. Now, you'd better leave. We've got a busy day ahead of us tomorrow."

He didn't argue, for which she was glad. His steps might have lagged a bit; she wasn't sure. It took barely two of his long strides to reach the door that connected their rooms. Bren waited only for it to close behind him before rushing over and clicking the lock in place.

6

Day five: Thursday
While the strategies we've listed are guaranteed to
help you land your man, the most important rule
is to be yourself. The second is to enjoy the re-
sults.

Land Your Man

Another sleepless night alone certainly showed that,
despite a knowledge of Bren's idiosyncrasies, Fletch
had not been a whopping success at winning her heart.
What he *had* managed to do was hurt her.

He had been privy to the sounds of her weeping via
the thin hotel wall that separated them. Longing to
comfort her and knowing she wouldn't accept his
shoulder to cry on had made for a bad night. Fletch
thought Bren had finally fallen asleep from exhaus-
tion, but the sound of movement next door around
dawn illustrated just how wrong he'd been. Attuned
to her every move now, he listened as bedsprings
sighed, suitcases were unzipped and zipped, shoes were
dropped and the shower run. Bren was out of her

room in less than ten minutes. Probably hurrying even more than usual to escape bumping into him, delaying the moment when she would be forced to see his mug again.

Tough, Fletch thought, hands behind his head as he stared at the ceiling. She was going to start seeing his face daily, from morning coffee to bedtime hot chocolate. It was going to be the last thing she saw each night and the first thing she blinked at every morning. And she was going to enjoy every second she spent with him for the rest of her life.

Funny how all it had taken was that shot about his marrying Dominique to clarify in his mind that marriage was exactly what he did want. Only with Bren as his bride.

Once he cleared up the misunderstanding that she was nothing more than a challenge to him—although winning her certainly was that—it would be smooth sailing. Straight to the altar, with no scenic sidetrips.

The key was to act natural and court her at the same time. Fletch was pretty sure he knew how she'd treat him—it would be all-business, something he'd rather avoid. And would. The trade show officially opened at ten, which left him almost four hours to come up with a decent con job. A tight schedule, but feasible for a very determined man.

When Fletch left the hotel an hour later, he was whistling.

Mick looked past Bren's shoulder when she showed up at the Bailey and Salazar booth a little after 8:00 a.m. "Where's Mr. Wonderful?"

"No idea," she admitted, hoping that the bucketful of ice she'd used had reduced the puffiness around her eyes. Slowly she removed her dark glasses, waiting for her co-workers to make some comment. No one did. Which either meant they hadn't noticed how haggard she looked or had made a pact not to say one word about her appearance. She didn't think the cold compresses, eyedrops and intensive use of makeup had cloaked the evidence of her crying jag all that well.

"Layton is planning to show up, isn't he?" Steve asked.

"He'll be here," Bren promised. "He's flaky but he isn't that flaky. He's got a vice presidency riding on this trip."

"I heard about that," Kurt said. "But I thought it was just an invention of the rumor mill. Isn't Layton kinda young for that kind of promotion?"

Bren shrugged. "Who am I to question the top-rungers? They never ask peons like us who should sit in those chairs, do they? Besides, Fletch actually does deserve a vice presidency—just don't tell him I said so, okay?"

"Honest to a fault," Steve moaned, shaking his head sadly. "Tell me, Bren, is there anything Layton can do to turn you against him?"

It was simply because she was so damn honest that Bren knew the answer to that one. "He's my best friend and has been for most of my life. I could never be mad at him for long."

"But you do get mad at him?" Kurt pressed.

"Frequently," Bren admitted, then turned her attention to the booth. "Now, have we got everything set for when the doors open? Promotional fliers?"

"Check," Steve announced, tapping the neat pile on the table with his hand and the box of extras under the table with his foot, before abandoning any business-related talk. "He bushwhacked us, you know."

Mick swung one of the rented metal folding chairs around and straddled it. "We considered having our stomachs pumped after downing that fire-eater chili he got us for lunch yesterday," he said. "Probably should have been suspicious when Layton didn't eat any of it himself."

Bren couldn't help herself. "He didn't eat anything?" she queried.

"Well, he inhaled that cherry thing he got for you," Kurt said.

"An empanada?"

"Said he needed a sugar hit," Steve muttered. "Think we're safe eating anything he orders for us today?"

"Maybe we should take turns and leave the premises for lunch. That way he can't slip us a mickey or anything," Kurt suggested.

"Good idea," Mick murmured. "Frankly, I wouldn't trust that dude as far as I can throw him."

"Which isn't far, considering he's got four inches and at least twenty pounds on you," Steve said.

Bren put her hands on her hips and glared at them. "Oh, give me a break. Fletch isn't that bad."

"She's right," Fletch announced, appearing behind her.

Bren tensed at the sound of his voice. He looked wonderful, she thought. His hair was groomed to a mahogany sheen, his wheat-colored, linen sports jacket set off the white of his dress shirt and the ivory of his immaculate slacks. Where the other men had worn company-issue brown ties with the Bailey and Salazar logo repeated in a small, sedate-looking maroon pattern, Fletch's neckwear was a warm gold emblazoned with wide, keyboardlike white smiles.

He was grinning one of his own. "I'm always painted worse than I actually am," he assured them. "Morning, all. Everybody religiously using Fresh All Day?"

Steve sat down quickly on another of the folding chairs. "Damn!" he muttered. "He got the name right."

"Will miracles never cease?" Kurt asked.

"How could he help but get it right?" Mick demanded, swinging his arm wide to indicate the B and S booth. "We're surrounded by signs that have Fresh All Day plastered all over them."

"Glad to see you, too, guys," Fletch said smoothly. "Anyone for breakfast?" He lifted a silvery bag.

"You eating whatever's in there, too?" Kurt asked suspiciously.

Fletch removed a long, thin box from the sack, opened it and offered it to Bren first. "Absolutely," he announced. "Actually, I thought we might all eat the same stuff today. You know, things like salad with garlic dressing, hoagies with pastrami and salami, pizza with pepperoni and onions. And we let everyone who stops by know what we ate."

"These are chocolates," Bren said. "Fletch, it isn't even nine yet."

"Didn't you get any dark chocolate?" Mick asked, peering at the selection.

"Bren is a milk-chocolate kind of woman," Fletch told him. "You really should know that if you're planning to hit on her."

At the flippant comment, Bren breathed easier. This was the Fletch she knew, not the stranger who'd kissed her last night like he never wanted to stop.

"Yeah," she agreed, helping herself to the candy. "Wise up, Mick. Shouldn't we be toasting the success of our product with champagne, though?"

Fletch's eyebrows flew upward in exaggerated surprise. "Drink on the job?"

"Forget I mentioned it," she said.

"Actually, the local chocolate company makes liqueur candies as well, and I've got a box with your name on it back at the hotel if you're interested later on," Fletch said. He offered the box around. "Anyone else?"

Kurt helped himself to a piece, but waited until Fletch popped one in his own mouth before eating it. "So the plan is to breathe on everyone to show Fresh All Day works the way we say it does?"

"In a nutshell, yes," Fletch said. "And if I remember correctly, you smoke, don't you, Mick?"

"I've tried to quit," Mick mumbled apologetically.

"Don't try too hard today," Fletch suggested. "In fact, I want you to nip out for quick drags frequently. We need to do any and all things we can think of to prove the damn toothpaste is as wonderful as the sign claims. Any questions?"

"Just one," Mick said. "Considering you actually want me to smoke, where do I go to vote you into that vice president's chair, Layton?"

Bren waited until the rest of the team was occupied before approaching Fletch. "Here," she murmured. "You need to wear your ID card."

"Promise not to stick me with the pin?" he asked lightly.

"Not if I can help it," she said, careful to keep her eyes on his lapel as she attached the card.

Fletch shook his head. "Wrong answer, Bren. You were suppose to say, 'Not deep enough to draw blood,' or something like that."

"It isn't that easy to go back to the way things were before," she murmured quietly to the Windsor knot of his tie.

Fletch nudged her chin upward until her eyes met his. "I know. Just do your damnedest. By the way, you look very nice today," he said.

Rather than dress like a clone of the men, she'd managed to get a vest made of the brown B and S–logo fabric and wore it over a white blouse and slacks that were a soft eggshell color. For comfort she'd opted for flats and stockings, both the same shade as oatmeal.

"Thanks," Bren said. "I really like your tie."

"It seemed appropriate." He glanced over her head to where show attendees had begun drifting down the aisle. "Looks like we're about to go on, sweetheart. Geared up to dish it out?"

"You mean hand out samples?"

Fletch grinned impishly. "I mean tell them whatever it takes to generate those gigantic orders the home office is counting on. Why else do you think they sent me?"

"To plague me?" Bren asked.

He chuckled. "That's my girl. Come on, watch the pro in action."

She was more than happy to tag along. It was a habit of long standing where Fletch was concerned.

Kurt had a live one. The woman's features were severe, as was her style of dressing, but she appeared to be melting under the timid smile of the hunky young Bailey and Salazar representative.

Fletch motioned for Bren to hang back and moved in himself, to hover at Kurt's shoulder.

The woman sorted through the brochures Kurt had given her. "The packaging is very attractive," she admitted, "but I doubt any toothpaste can do as much as you are claiming is possible."

"It's been tested thoroughly," Kurt assured her.

"Most thoroughly," Fletch agreed. "In fact, we're continuing to test it right here in the booth."

"Yes, we are," Kurt said. "We're all using Fresh All Day in the morning, and I can personally attest to the fact that none of us has used a mouthwash of any kind at any time during the day. The toothpaste continues to kill bacteria that causes bad breath for up to twelve hours."

"Some users swear to more than that," Fletch added.

"You would say that," the woman insisted. "You work for the company, don't you?"

"If you can term something this enjoyable as work," Fletch said. "But rather than take our word for it, why don't you test Fresh All Day yourself?"

"I already have a sample," she said.

Fletch grinned widely. "I wasn't talking about using it, but of testing us."

Kurt glanced back at Bren, but she shrugged, just as lost as he was.

"Lean forward," Fletch urged the woman. "Nose to nose with my associate here. Now, Kurt, say 'halitosis hardly ever happens.'"

Kurt did as instructed.

"No, no. More like Eliza Doolittle. Huff your *H*s," Fletch said.

"*Hal*itosis *hard*ly ever *hap*pens," Kurt gasped out.

"Mmm. Minty," the woman said. "But it's still early in the day."

"Oh, Kurt's not going anywhere," Fletch assured her. "Stop back by later, after the garlic bread arrives."

Bren stepped up next to Kurt as the woman moved on to the next booth. "She won't be back," she said.

Fletch chuckled. "Weren't you listening? That was a five-thousand-dollar sale, my darling."

A bit distracted at being called his darling, Bren was glad when Kurt exploded. "What are you talking about?" he demanded. "I was standing right here and never heard one word about money."

"Nevertheless, it was our first sale of the day," Fletch insisted. "The lady is a buyer for a pharmaceutical retailer in the northwest. Five thousand is pretty conservative, considering how many outlets her company has. When she comes back, remember, halitosis hardly ever happens. Make sure you tell her what you had for lunch, too."

Fletch moved off as more visitors eased up to the booth. Kurt exchanged a puzzled look with Bren.

"Don't ask," she warned, "because I have no idea how he knows. Experience, maybe."

"Vice president, hmm?" Kurt mused. "Sure that's the title he's aiming for?"

"You think it should be president or chairman of the board?" Bren asked, her conversation with Dominique in mind.

"Naw," Kurt said. "I was thinking more along the lines of czar."

Bren joined Steve at the rear of the booth four hours later, her feet aching from standing on the concrete floor. As the other official member from the sales department, Steve was eating pizza as he busily tallied amounts on the orders they'd already taken for Fresh All Day.

"So what's the total so far?" she asked, sinking thankfully into the chair next to him.

Steve didn't bother to glance up, but continued punching numbers into his hand-held calculator. "About $100,000, which is seed money, but not much more."

"Seed money?" Bren repeated.

"The big orders are yet to come in," he explained, tossing a piece of pepperoni into his mouth.

Fletch hunkered down next to Bren. "And we need some pretty hefty ones at that," he said. "Time for the flanking movement."

"That sounds awfully military," Bren complained. "Couldn't we just call it Plan B?"

"You're Plan B," Fletch said, dropping his hand casually on her thigh, then snatching it away as if he'd been burned.

He was still as overly sensitive as she was, Bren figured. That wildly passionate kiss had changed everything between them. Their casual camaraderie had burned to cinders in the flames of desire. No matter how much they pretended it hadn't happened, it had, and there was no going back.

"What exactly is involved in this particular flanking movement?" Steve asked.

"Circumlocution," Fletch said. "If a prospective customer asks if Fresh All Day has fluoride, baking soda or peroxide like the competitors' brands do, what do you say?"

"No," Bren answered. "It doesn't."

Fletch pointed his index finger at Steve.

"It doesn't *yet*," the sales rep said. "As we speak, chemists are working to combine these popular elements with the breath-control properties of Fresh All Day."

"They are?" Bren gasped.

"I have no idea," Fletch admitted, "but it is the logical step to take, isn't it?"

"Well, yes," she said. "But isn't saying so without knowing for sure lying?"

"Circumlocution," Fletch insisted. "And as far as we know, we aren't lying, right, Steve?"

"B-but—" Bren sputtered.

"Don't believe in your pet product, sweetheart?" Fletch teased lightly.

Steve wiped grease from his fingers, then slipped his calculator back in his shirt pocket. He tossed a sample package of Fresh All Day to Bren. She jerked back in her chair, catching it between her hands.

"How do we know they aren't working on the new improved version, Bren?" Steve asked.

"Well..."

"We don't. But all we have to do is report back that our customers were interested in adding fluoride and all that, and chances are they'll turn up as highly touted additions within the year," he said. "It's happened before."

"In fact, I'll give you odds that product development withheld those elements for the launch just so they'd have an advertising coup when the timing is right," Fletch added.

"Good point," Steve murmured, sounding impressed.

Fletch stood up, pulling Bren with him. "Come on, I'll show you how it's done," he offered, "just in case you ever decide to transfer to sales."

Shaking her head slowly, Bren slipped her hand from his and sat down again. "Pass," she said. "Think I'll just eat my salad and observe from a distance."

"Sure?" Fletch asked.

"More than sure," Bren said, reaching for her lunch.

Steve followed him and soon both men were chatting to prospective customers, laying on the charm with a trowel.

Kurt stumbled into the chair Steve had abandoned, staring back over his shoulder in surprise. "Do you know what Mr. Wonderful just told that guy?" he demanded.

"Something we never heard in advertising?" Bren murmured, taking a sip of soda to wash the taste of garlic dressing away. The stuff was so strong, she wondered if Fresh All Day was going to be able to combat it sufficiently to woo customers to the product.

"Layton said there was a Fresh All Day version for sensitive teeth in the works," Kurt said. "You hear anything about it?"

Bren lifted her shoulders in a giant shrug. "No. But you know, Kurt," she mused, "there really should be one, shouldn't there?"

As he assured the procession of visitors that Fresh All Day was unlike any other toothpaste in the world, Fletch could feel his palm still burning from contact with Bren's thigh. Or, more important, from the very distinctive feel of a garter clip beneath the fabric of her slacks. The impression was seared in his memory, in his mind. And it was wreaking havoc with his equilibrium.

The vision of Bren in a garter belt and stockings danced in his head. He'd never envisioned her in such erotic lingerie. She seemed more the flannel-pajamas-and-cotton-underwear type. A guy didn't naturally associate exotic scraps of lace and ribbon with the champion shortstop on his softball team.

Of course, Bren had been surprising him quite a bit lately. Jolting him into a new awareness of her. There'd been that little slip of a dress she'd worn the night he took her dancing, then the even briefer, sexier one last night, which drew attention to her creamy skin and narrow waist. In the last few days, he'd gandered enough tempting glimpses of thigh and other feminine delights to wonder why he'd let so much time go by before noticing she had grown into a beauty. Today she had reverted to her regular style, going back to the mannish-cut blouses and trousers she'd worn to work every day for the last four years. But underneath the conservative facade...oh, Lord. Their shared past had lured him into thinking he really knew her, when the fact of the matter was he knew very little about Bren the woman.

But he was going to enjoy every minute of getting to know her. Winning her. And there was no time like the present to begin.

"Just how quickly does this stuff work?" the visitor before him asked. "I mean, it's midafternoon now. Supposedly a person would brush at, say, seven in the morning. That's a good seven hours, with lunch sandwiched in there somewhere. If I'm going into a meeting with an important client, will I feel confident about my breath?"

Fletch grinned and glanced back to where Bren sat, feet up on the spare chair, a plastic fork loaded with salad halfway to her lips. He waited until the fork was empty before signaling to her. She gulped hastily, trying to finish chewing her mouthful of food as she put her lunch aside and got up to join him.

"That's a very interesting question," Fletch said. "But I think, with the help of my lovely associate here, we can ease your mind about the effectiveness of Fresh All Day. Bren, why don't you tell this gentleman what you were eating."

She hid her mouth briefly with her hand, hastily swallowing the last of her meal. "It was fairly simple," she insisted, offering the prospective customer a bright toothpaste smile. "The dressing was lethal, though. Here, I've got a dab on my finger. Can you smell the garlic?"

The buyer bent forward and sniffed obediently before reeling back. "I'll say that's strong."

"Now for the true test," Bren announced, and leaned toward him. Fletch noticed she crossed her fingers behind her back before breathing his catch phrase, "*Hal*itosis *hard*ly ever *hap*pens."

"Say that again," the man urged.

Bren did as requested.

He lifted the small sample box of Fresh All Day. "And when was the last time you used this stuff?"

Bren glanced at Fletch. "Well, I was up fairly early today. It was about six, I guess."

"You haven't used it again since?"

She chuckled. "You don't know this taskmaster," Bren told him, indicating Fletch. "He hasn't let me out of this booth since the show opened this morning. Before then, we were too busy getting ready to have a moment to breathe, much less brush our teeth again.''

The man looked impressed. "Eight hours, hmm?"

"And she's still kissing fresh, right?" Fletch asked.

The customer—Fletch was sure the order was as good as written—laughed. "Well, I wouldn't know about that."

"I'll find out for you," Fletch offered, slipping his arm around Bren's waist. "Plan B," he murmured before brushing his mouth over hers.

Bren gasped lightly but didn't protest. She even rose up on her toes, her lips clinging a moment.

"Mmm, minty still," Fletch announced and turned back to his amused client. "Actually, I think she had the tamer lunch. Care to hear what I ate?"

"Why don't you tell me how soon the first shipment can be in my warehouse instead?" the man countered.

Plan B was the standard pitch the rest of the day, although only for Fletch. When Mick asked if he could use it, he was told he could only if he found his own woman.

"It's a tricky ploy," Fletch explained. "There's all that sexual harassment stuff to get around. Fortunately, Bren knows there's nothing personal in this. We're simply doing a demonstration, rather like a couple kissing in a commercial. Right, sweetheart?"

Bren was tempted to point out that calling her "sweetheart" wasn't a very good way to illustrate there wasn't a lick of sexual intent in the kisses. And, if Fletch actually believed what he said, he was lying to himself, because every kiss he gave her built on the one before, each more ardent than the last. He was seducing her by millimeters in front of their co-workers and a convention center full of strangers. There were no tender words she might later question for sincerity. There was no hot-handed groping, no hugs, no touching her hair, no nuzzling her ears. Only brief blendings of their mouths, their breath.

It was intoxicating. Exciting. Wonderful. And the only time in her life that she would ever feel mind-stoppingly special.

She wasn't brain numb enough to think the sensation would last. Fletch was simply reminding her that a physical awareness existed and could—not necessarily should or would but *could*—be acted upon. The idea was extremely seductive. Even if she later regretted giving in to the impulse, Bren surrendered to it and began kissing him back.

It was nearly time for the trade show to close its doors for the day when things not only went downhill, but pitched right off a steep cliff.

Steve's latest total put the orders near the million-dollar mark for the day. The seed money had grown as quickly as Jack's bean stalk. Although Bren knew the sales figures on personal-care products were hefty, she was still amazed at the size of the orders the various warehouses placed. And they were only the opening orders, Fletch hastened to explain. There were two days of the show remaining. He hoped another million and a half would be written in that time, and fully expected subsequent orders would be placed within a couple of weeks for another five million.

"Actually, the orders we got today don't really reflect our wonderful sales techniques," he told her during a break in the stream of visitors. "The promotion schedule pretty much demands that the big suppliers carry Fresh All Day. Their customers will be coming in with coupons clipped from all the major magazines and Sunday newspaper supplements. They'll see Fresh All Day TV spots between the daytime soaps and sandwiched among their favorite prime-time shows. Retailers will be clambering to fill the early demand for the stuff."

"So why exactly are we circumlo-whatevering and executing Plan B?" Bren asked.

"Because it's fun," Fletch said, grinning lazily down at her. "Lots of fun."

He was right about that, Bren decided. She hadn't been looking forward to the day at all, but now she didn't particularly want it to end.

"These claims are pretty fantastic," her current customer murmured, looking over the full-color, trifold brochure Bren had helped design and execute. "Up to twelve hours of bacteria control? Tell me truthfully, when did you last use the product?"

"At six this morning," Bren said. "And we've been eating some pretty awful stuff throughout the day."

"And remained kissing fresh, as I understand it."

Bren chuckled. "The demonstrations have got us some attention," she admitted.

"And made the day go by much faster," Fletch added, turning up at her elbow. "It's almost as great as filling your order will be."

The customer laughed. "I would have hoped for this young lady's sake that it would be better than that."

"Quality-control problems, you think?" he asked flippantly. "Bren, perhaps you'd better have another breath analysis."

"If you insist." She glanced up at him, eyes dancing with anticipation—and caught sight of Dominique sashaying through the crowd toward the Bailey and Salazar booth.

Bren's world imploded. She couldn't let Fletch's self-destruct, though. Rather than turn naturally into his arms as she had done all afternoon, Bren spun to where Mick stood, yanked on his tie to drag him forward and kissed him long and hard.

Fletch stood rooted to the spot, staring in disbelief at the woman he loved.

Bren whirled back to face her customer. "Mick here is a smoker who has been trying to stop but has indulged today in—how many cigarettes, Mick?" she asked.

"Half a pack," Mick croaked, although whether it was from the shock of Bren's kiss or from near strangulation by his tie, Fletch couldn't tell. Perhaps both.

The smile Bren turned on her still-stunned coworker was dazzling. "That many? Well, I sure didn't taste anything but Fresh All Day's pleasant mint flavoring," she insisted, the beam of her smile redirected to her customer as she leaned forward. "In fact, not long ago I had an order of nachos with jalapeño cheese...."

Fletch didn't catch the rest of Bren's spiel. Another voice distracted him, sent his well-ordered plans tipping over in confusion.

"Hello, Fletcher," Dominique cooed hotly across the meager barricade of the front table. "Surprised to see me?"

"*Surprised* wouldn't be the word I'd use," he said. At least Bren's strange behavior was now explained. She hadn't wanted to kiss him in front of his former girlfriend.

Because Bren didn't realize how former a girlfriend Dominique was.

Neither did she.

"Pleased then?" Dominique suggested.

That wasn't exactly how he was feeling, either, Fletch thought. *Angry* fit pretty damn well, though. He could see all his patient work convincing Bren that he was in earnest disappearing as quickly as Bren's high school beaux had when they'd caught sight of him bird-dogging.

"I know you still have a couple of days before you give me an answer, darling," Dominique purred, "but I couldn't wait at home alone, knowing you were missing me."

"Actually, I've been swamped," Fletch said. "All those preliminary things, then getting here, setting up, selling. You understand, Dominique. I haven't had time to, uh . . ."

"Call me?" she suggested, when his voice trailed off as if he was stumped.

Fletch glanced over to where Mick sat looking as bug-eyed as a fish out of water, while Bren helped him loosen his tie. Steve was busy writing up an order for Bren's customer. Kurt stood off to the side, tilting back a can of soda pop. When Fletch jogged his arm, diet cola slopped over the rim and dribbled down Kurt's chin.

"Listen, I can't get away," Fletch told Dominique, "but Kurt here can be spared. He'll not only be happy to take you back to your hotel, he's free to be your tour guide tonight. Isn't that right, Kurt?"

Mopping hastily at his chin, Kurt stared at Fletch, then at Dominique, then back at Fletch. "You're kidding . . . ah, I mean, sure. No problem."

Dominique smiled thinly. Not a bit of warmth reached her eyes, Fletch noted. Had it ever? Bren's eyes mirrored her emotions, sparkling when she was happy, warming when she was pleased about something and glowing when she was in his arms.

And he'd almost overlooked her. Bren. The best thing that had ever happened to him.

Talk about having one hell of a close call!

"How sweet of you to offer," Dominique murmured, giving Kurt a look that clearly said she'd rather slop hogs than be seen with him. Poor Kurt, Fletch thought. He had muscles and looks but lacked a glowing future, the one requirement Dominique insisted her men possess.

"But it's not a problem for me to wait until you finish up here," Dominique assured Fletch. "Don't the doors close in another thirty minutes?"

He hadn't realized she was such a master of strategy before. It was going to take fast footwork to avoid a claustrophobic seizure after that flanking movement, Fletch decided.

"My evening is even more tied up than my day has been," he murmured vaguely. "Orders and stuff."

Steve finished with the latest customer and glanced over his shoulder. "Oh, that's in the bag, Layton. I've been keeping everything up to snuff as we go. All I've got to do is fax the orders into headquarters tonight, which shouldn't take but half an hour at the most. You're free as a bird."

Fletch wondered if it was possible to reassign Steve to a sales district in the vast, relatively unpopulated stretches of the central Nevada desert. "Thanks," he snarled.

"Hey, my pleasure," Steve insisted with a grin that showed he knew exactly how little his offer was appreciated. He compounded the issue by adding, "Thought I'd ask Bren if she'd like to see the Las Vegas Stars game with me tonight."

The two tickets Fletch had to the game burned in his trouser pocket. Forget the desert. He was going to send Steve to the polar region, the farther north the better. When Fletch was done with his cohort, the only customers the man was likely to have were Santa's elves.

"Say, where is Bren, anyway?" Steve asked. "She was here a minute ago."

She was probably in cowardly retreat, Fletch reflected. Like he'd prefer to be.

Mick's eyes weren't protruding as prominently, although his company tie had been yanked loose and was off center, and his hair looked like he'd been pulling at it in frustration. Fletch knew the sensation only too well at the moment.

"Bren gathered up her purse and a basket of samples to distribute to the crowd. Claimed she'd be back to help us straighten up when the doors close," Mick said.

"I'll go look for her," Steve said.

Fletch snagged the salesman's arm before he could get away. "No, you help Kurt show Dominique around the show," he suggested. "You deserve a break, and now's as good a time as any to take it."

"How considerate," Steve murmured sarcastically. "Bren *will* be here when I get back, won't she?"

Fletch shrugged. "Who's to say?" he asked, mentally calculating how he could keep Steve away from Bren, Dominique away from Bren and still retain his sanity. "Better hurry or there won't be much to see."

Bracketed between the two men, Dominique twisted to wiggle her fingers at him as she slinked down the aisle.

Fletch waited until the crowd shielded him from Dominique's eagle eye should she glance back. "You're in charge," he said to Mick, and vaulted over the table.

"Me?" Mick croaked, correctly identifying his new status as a punishment. "What did I do?"

"Enjoyed Plan B," Fletch growled. "Which way did Bren go?"

Mick pointed, thankfully in the opposite direction from the one Dominique and her escorts had taken. Fletch took off running.

* * *

Bren's smile was plastered on her face as she moved through the throng of show visitors. She stopped frequently, passing out the small sample sizes of Fresh All Day from the basket on her arm, but her mind wasn't on pushing the toothpaste. It was on Dominique's sudden appearance.

Had Fletch's intended become impatient? Had she regretted giving him a deadline and come to patch things up with him?

Had he called her and asked her to come to Vegas?

Bren's heart sank. What else had she expected? It had been only last night when he'd told her he hoped to be married by Monday. She had been expecting him to make Dominique his bride ever since Sunday, when he'd confided in Bren, giving her the ultimatum note to read.

You're stupid, Brenda Burton, Bren lectured herself silently. *You knew all he was doing was playing, entertaining himself with you, but still you let yourself dream. Let yourself enjoy every minute, every caress, every kiss.*

She would cherish the memory of them. Instead of thinking of him as her childhood playmate, her best friend, he would now become the lover who got away. She should be glad that Dominique had shown up and put a stop to the silliness, the hopelessness. Should be. But all Bren could think about was what might have happened if Fletch's girlfriend *hadn't* shown up. Would Bren have allowed him to become her lover in truth that night? Knowing he belonged elsewhere, she shouldn't have considered that an option, but she'd been seesawing over the decision since the first tender Plan B kiss of the day.

There wasn't any reason to dwell on it anymore. Even with the help of *Land Your Man,* there was no way a fellow would ever choose her over the sexy Dominique. Not a sane one, at least. Bren wasn't the kind of woman men lusted over, despite the nice lies Mick, Kurt and Steve had told her. She'd learned that lesson long ago, back when she landed her first short-stop position and truly became "one of the guys." Her interests had always been those shared by her male friends, and her friends had nearly always been male. Still were.

Now she was losing her best friend because there was no way she could go back to a strictly platonic relationship with Fletch Layton. His kisses and her dreams were standing firmly in the way.

Not to mention Dominique, his bride-to-be.

Damn Sally and her dumb book. Bren had almost begun to believe Fletch had fallen in love with her.

"Hey, it's the Kissing Fresh girl," a man said. Nudging his friend, he gestured toward Bren.

The toothpaste was doomed, she thought. Not only did the staffers at Bailey and Salazar have trouble remembering the official name, now even the consumers couldn't get it right.

Bren gave the two men her best Fresh All Day smile. "Would you like some samples to take home for your families?" she asked.

"Actually, what I'd like is to see just how kissing fresh you are, honey," the first man said.

"I'll take a sample, too, sugar, but not another tube of toothpaste," his friend added, closing in on her.

Around them visitors streamed toward the doors, too tired to notice the building situation. Bren looked frantically for a security guard, but there was none in sight.

"I'm sorry, gentlemen, but the only samples I'm giving out are these," she said, trying to thrust the tiny toothpaste tubes into their hands.

The first man accepted the sample, but the second let his fall to the floor and slipped his arm around her waist. "Show me what a great job it does and I'll take all of them off your hands, sugar," he said.

Bren fought down a wave of panic. *Think,* she urged her brain. Smack him with the basket. Kick him in the shins. Deck him. Damn, why hadn't she ever taken up one of the martial arts?

His arm tightened, pulling her closer. Bren felt engulfed in a cloud of alcoholic fumes. Since he was soused, reasoning with him was definitely not an option. Smashing his toes was.

Trying to twist away from the man, she raised her foot to stomp him good.

And nearly lost her balance as his presence was abruptly removed.

"The lady isn't interested, pal," Fletch snarled, his voice icy. "Beat it before I forget where we are."

"Just wanted a private demonstration," the drunk insisted, shrugging Fletch off. "Hell, you been hoggin' her all to yourself, buddy. Your mother never tell you it's better to share?"

Fletch's hand flashed out, gathering a fistful of the man's shirt. "Yours ever mention the words *sexual harassment?*" he snapped.

"Hey, we didn't mean nothing, mister," the first man insisted, trying to extricate his friend from Fletch's grip. "We saw you kissing her and thought—"

"You thought wrong," Fletch growled, and gave his hapless opponent a push as he released him. "The lady is engaged to marry me."

Bren choked back a gasp at the outright lie.

The men stumbled, one falling against the other. "Sorry. We didn't know," the more sober one said.

"She's not wearing a ring, you know?" the drunk mumbled, as if that excused his actions.

Together they hastily shuffled out of the building.

Bren gaped at Fletch. He was still coldly furious, she could tell. She'd forgotten he possessed this darker side. It surfaced so infrequently and it had been so long since she'd seen it. He'd been twelve at the time.

It had been at one of the ball games leading to the championship play-offs, she remembered. The umpire had called Fletch out at home plate. Although he'd stolen home, he'd been safe by a mile and everyone but the ump seemed to know it.

Fletch had had the same look in his eyes that day at the ballpark that he wore now. Back then the ump had stepped back a pace as if he feared the furious boy. Bren figured the men who had accosted her were lucky Fletch had let them leave under their own power. The only other option would have been via an ambulance.

She touched his arm gently. "Thank you," she said.

Fletch came back to earth, his expression clearing to the easygoing one she was used to seeing. "Knight errantry has always been a hobby of mine where you are concerned," he said flippantly. "I think it's time you got out of here."

"Can't. Too much to do back at the booth," Bren insisted. "And you've got Dominique to see to. I'll be okay now."

"Will you ever learn to take orders without arguing?" Fletch asked. Putting a forceful hand on her elbow, he pushed her toward the exit. "We can handle things. You head back to the hotel. Relax around the pool, but try not to talk to any strangers, hmm, little girl? Too damn many wolves around for my peace of mind."

Bren tried to drag her feet. "Fletch, I—"

He fished in his trouser pocket. "Here. I'd hoped we could enjoy ourselves at Cashman Field tonight, but that was before complications arose." He slipped the tickets for the ball game into her hand.

"Complications?" Bren squawked. "Dominique is a little more than a complication, Fletch. She's the woman you're going to marry."

"I know who I'm going to marry," he said, pushing through the convention-center doors. "Maybe you can find someone to go to the game with you. Kurt, maybe. He seems relatively safe."

"Why not Mick?" she asked.

"He hasn't recovered from that smacker you laid on him," Fletch explained.

"Steve then."

Fletch put his fingers to his mouth and whistled shrilly for a taxi. "He was too willing to start a line behind Mick," he said.

"You can get off the knight-errant kick," Bren said with a sigh. "I think I'll just buy a paperback novel and soak in the tub. It sounds safer." She handed the tickets back to him. "Here, take Dominique to the game."

"No, thanks. But if you're sure you don't want to go, I'll find someone to palm them off on."

A cab zipped up to the curb. The driver leaned toward his open side window. "Where to, folks?"

Fletch pulled the back door open.

"You'll do what I suggested? Swim, relax, not talk to strangers?"

Just act as if nothing had happened between them? Pretend that Dominique wasn't enjoying every fantasy Bren herself had had over the past few days? Oh, sure, she'd relax real well, she decided bitterly.

Trying to put their relationship back on its old footing, Bren saluted. "Aye, aye, sir."

"You're a terrible liar, Bren," Fletch murmured. Then he kissed her. Not as he'd been doing all afternoon, those sweet, tender, patient caresses, but as he'd kissed her the night before in the elevator.

Bren's knees nearly buckled.

"Stay out of trouble," he ordered softly as she sank back in the taxi, the basket of samples still hooked over her arm.

"Right," Bren murmured, dazed. As far as she was concerned, she already was in trouble. Big trouble.

7

Day six: Friday

You've used every strategy, every ploy we've suggested and he's still resisting? Don't worry. Like various varieties of fish, some men are harder to land than others. If you truly feel he's worth the effort you've expended, your persistence will pay off in the end.

Land Your Man

Fletch woke early, his mind whirling with plans. Now if things only turned out the way he wanted them to, life would be good.

If not...

It wasn't something he could contemplate without a shiver of revulsion.

Throwing back the covers, he palmed the phone and put phase one into operation, then headed for the shower.

They really should give out Academy Awards for performances in real life, he mused, thinking back over the evening before. Rather than waste perfectly good seats to the ball game on his and Bren's co-workers, Fletch, after watching Bren's taxi whisk her away, had hunted down the buyers for Tanglewood Wholesalers. They'd placed an opening order for a quarter of a million and deserved to be rewarded. At least more so than Mick, considering he'd been kissed by Bren, or Steve, who'd wanted to, or Kurt, who...well, who had once had the temerity to ask her out.

Fletch's return to the booth coincided with Dominique's, not allowing sufficient time to concoct a new alibi. So he fell back on one she'd used in the past.

"You have what?" Dominique had snapped, eyes flashing with fury.

Fletch hoped the guys back home never learned of what he was about to do. If they did, he'd never live it down.

"A headache." He rubbed his temple fretfully for effect. "I'm entitled, believe me," he insisted. Perhaps he'd whined, Fletch reflected. At any rate, Dominique had backed off, accepting Steve as a substitute escort for the evening. She hadn't offered to nurse Fletch back to health like Bren would have.

Dominique might be one of the most beautiful women to ever drape herself over his arm, but she had a heart of tungsten steel. Bren's, on the other hand, melted as quickly as ice cream on a summer's day. If he'd let her stick around to hear the excuse he'd bleated, chances were she would have offered him aspirins, cold cloths and enough other cure-all suggestions to prove she'd be a wonderful mother.

Now there was an idea to set a man back on his heels. Bren as a mother. He could see her now, Fletch thought as he stepped out of the shower, toweling off. Her pretty chestnut curls tossed in adorable disorder, her gorgeous green eyes soft and tender as she bent over his child...

The towel froze in his hand. The vanity mirror was steamed up, which was a blessing. He couldn't see how far his jaw had dropped.

"Back up a step, Layton," Fletch ordered out loud. Motherhood for Bren. It sounded right. It sounded good. But if things went as he hoped, that meant fatherhood for himself.

Fatherhood. Bouncing his daughter on his knee. Teaching her to hold a bat just right to knock a ball over the outfield fence. Bren would teach her the finer points of being a shortstop. And when it came time for her to attend her high school prom—well, he'd turn over protection duties to her brother, a handsome young man with Fletch's build and Bren's eyes.

Yeah, fatherhood, he mused happily. It had one hell of a fine ring to it.

Now all he had to do was place a few more calls, brush Dominique off, wrap up the trade show on a successful note and close the deal with Bren.

He had a feeling the last one was going to demand all his finesse. And, if necessary, a tumble between the sheets. A man had to do what a man had to do.

He'd just shrugged into his sports coat when there was a knock on the hall door. Fletch glanced at his watch. "Right on time," he said as he opened the door.

"I am?" Dominique purred throatily. "I didn't even know you were expecting me, darling." She snaked her arms around his neck, leaning her voluptuous body into his. "Headache all gone?"

Fletch started to get one in truth.

He pulled her hands from his nape, forcing distance between them. "Haven't you forgotten something?" he asked.

Dominique tilted her head to the side. "Oh, you don't mean that depressing trade show, do you? I'm sure they can do without you a bit longer, Fletcher. Brenda is so competent and efficient, I'm sure she can handle things without you there."

And if Brenda heard Dominique's voice through the still-locked connecting door, his ship was truly sunk.

"I mean your nasty little note," Fletch said. "It clearly states, I believe, that if I have no intention of marrying you, you never want to see me again."

Dominique pouted. "You didn't think I meant that literally, did you?" She tried to walk her fingers teasingly up his lapel.

Fletch caught her wrist and plucked it away. "Oh, yes, I did," he said, deadly serious. "And you did mean exactly that, Dominique. Last Sunday. You only showed up here because you hadn't heard from me and were afraid you'd gone too far."

She snatched her wrist from his encircling fingers. "What are you trying to tell me, Fletcher? That you don't want to marry me?" Dominique slid her palms down over her hips. "That you don't want this body anymore?"

Another knock sounded on the door. "That's exactly what I'm saying," Fletch said, stepping forward to answer the door again. This time it was the room-service cart he'd expected earlier.

White linen fluttered as the attendant wheeled it into the room. Deep red and warm gold rosebuds quivered in their vase, bobbing with the trolley's movement. Domed silver covers protected the entrées. Fletch signed the room tab and passed a tip to the waiter, sending him on his way quickly. He didn't close the door behind the man, though.

Dominique didn't take the hint. Instead, her eyes narrowed as she noted exactly how many dishes were being delivered. "I see." Her tone rivaled the temperature of an arctic weather front. "It isn't hard to guess just who has taken advantage of this situation. Brenda's fancied herself in love with you for years. This was probably the only chance she'd ever have to get you to herself." Dominique's upper lip curved in a sneer. "You'll break her heart, of course, but what do I care?"

"Exactly," Fletch said. "What do you care? And now I think it is past time for you to leave, Dominique. Make the most of your visit and see if you can't find another sucker in one of the casinos before you leave."

If she'd been a cat, she would have hissed and spat at him as she moved past him and out the door, her hips working overtime in a last-ditch effort to show him what he was throwing away.

Fletch let the door close softly behind her. Dominique was a truly gorgeous woman—physically rather than spiritually—but she wasn't his best friend. A very special lady already held that title and had for an incredibly long time. She was loyal, daring, honest and the sexiest creature he'd ever known. And he'd been incredibly stupid not to have seen it long before.

Wheeling the room-service cart over to the connecting door, Fletch did a shave-and-a-haircut rap on it. "Open up, Bren. Breakfast is getting cold," he announced loudly.

"Breakfast?" she called drowsily. Then the bedsprings creaked. "Just a minute."

His stomach twisted in knots as he waited. It was one thing to decide to propose, but one hell of another to actually go through with it, Fletch thought, his throat going dry suddenly. It got even drier when he heard the lock turn.

"I thought I heard Dominique," Bren said, pulling the door open.

Her curls were unraveling, some nearly flattened after being slept on. Her eyelashes fluttered with the effort to brush sleep aside. Tracks from crushed bed sheets marked one side of her face.

A face that looked pink and perfect to him.

As did the rest of her.

Bren pulled the front of her robe together to cover herself as she blinked at him, but, considering the garment was made of a bit of diaphanous peach silk and a good deal of lace, the action was pretty well useless. Beneath the robe there was more lace decorating the bodice of a short nightgown that dipped low over her breasts and ended high on her thighs.

An extremely pleasant jolt of adrenaline started Fletch's heart moving again.

"Dominique? Oh, she just stopped by to say goodbye," he said, and pushed the breakfast cart over the threshold and into her room.

"She's leaving already?" Bren started for the bathroom door. "Let me get dressed and—"

Fletch unveiled a plate of bacon, scrambled eggs and French toast. "Don't bother. Things will get cold."

Bren's willowy form weaved as if drawn by the heavenly scent of the bacon. Of course, Fletch thought, it could just be an illusion caused by that delightfully feminine getup.

She sat down at the table near the window, pushing the drapes open while Fletch slid the seductive plate of her favorites before her.

"You know, I would have pictured you as the kind of girl who slept in an old football jersey," he said.

"Oh, no," Bren insisted, already savoring a forkful of eggs. "I wear enough of that kind of stuff when I play sports. Stuff like this is, well, my secret weakness."

It was one of his, too. He was going to enjoy every second it took to peel it off of her. And so was Bren.

But first things first.

Fletch reached in his pocket, his fingers closing around the small jeweler's box secreted there. There was one very handy aspect of life in Las Vegas that he had discovered the evening before. The major hotels had jewelry stores on the premises that stayed open late for the convenience of any visitor who was fortunate enough to leave the casino a winner.

Or for desperate men in search of engagement rings.

"Did they send up maple syrup?" Bren asked, savoring a piece of bacon.

Fletch wondered if she knew it drove him a bit nuts to watch her hold the strip between her fingers as she sank her perfect little teeth into it.

"Syrup," he said, passing the small pitcher over as he settled into the chair across from hers. "You might want this, too." He tossed her the royal blue, velvet box.

As the excellent ball player that she was, Bren caught it one-handed. "What is it?"

"Just something I hope you'll wear today," Fletch murmured, cutting into the pile of pancakes on his own plate.

A puzzled frown creased her brow, but she did put her fork down to open the hinged lid.

He watched her, chewing automatically, not tasting a damn thing.

"Fletch!" she gasped.

"Like it?"

"It's beautiful, but far too expensive to use just so creeps like those yesterday don't bother me," Bren said. She snapped the box closed without touching the ring.

Fletch watched her place his offering on the table between them.

"Besides," she said, giving him a brave smile, "I don't think Dominique would appreciate me wearing her diamond before she got it."

Dominique again. Fletch gritted his teeth. "You didn't look at it very closely if you think that's the kind of ring Dominique would consider wearing."

"Why not?" Bren asked.

He rolled his eyes. There were definite drawbacks to being in love with a woman as innocent and well-intentioned as Bren was. "Not to insult you, my love, but the stone isn't big enough to interest Dominique."

"It isn't? It looked gigantic to me."

Bless her little heart. He was going to have to get her a larger diamond just because she was so unmercenary.

"I bought it with you in mind," Fletch said.

"You did?" Her eyes glowed, but she still hadn't picked up on what he was trying to tell her. Obviously subtlety wasn't going to work.

"Well, it's still far too expensive for a phony engagement," Bren said. "If you don't mind, I'll zip off to one of the malls and find a decent-looking fake for ten or twenty bucks. That should be enough to scare off any—"

Fletch grabbed the jeweler's box, yanked the ring from it and pushed himself to his feet. "You're wearing this one and that's the end of it."

As Bren stared at him in stunned silence, he rammed the ring on the third finger of her left hand. Then he sat back down and returned to his breakfast.

"Don't you dare mention another word about Dominique or getting a phony ring. I know which woman I want to marry and this damn diamond fits her perfectly!" he snarled, aiming a forkful of pancake at her before shoving it in his mouth.

She looked at him as if he'd lost his marbles. They were probably rolling around on the floor, Fletch decided, scattered to the four corners.

"But *I'm* wearing it," Bren insisted.

"Damn right," Fletch growled. "And if you take it off for any reason other than to get the matching wedding band on, you'll have me to deal with, sister."

"A matching wedding band?" she gasped. "But—"

Fletch sighed and put down his fork. "I'm asking you to marry me, Bren. Is that too hard to believe?"

She blinked at him. "Yes," she said, "it is."

It felt like she'd kicked him in the solar plexus. "You mean you don't want to marry me?" he croaked in disbelief.

Bren's lashes dipped over her eyes. She stared at her half-eaten breakfast. "No. I just can't believe that you want to marry me."

Well, damn!

Fletch sat staring at her for what felt like an eternity. Bren held her breath, barely daring to breathe. She was dreaming for sure, because it was only in her dreams that he looked at her this way. As if she were the only woman in the world. As if he was madly in love with her.

On her finger his ring—a diamond ring!—glittered in the sunlight that spilled into the room. The yellow gold of the band glowed warmly against her skin.

Fletch pushed his breakfast aside and got to his feet, taking her hand in is. Mesmerized, Bren stood up, suddenly very conscious of her apparel—or lack of it. Fletch's eyes were on her face, though. He guided her hand until it rested flat against his chest. The fabric of his shirt was cool to the touch but his skin quickly warmed her palm. The strong and steady pulsing of his heart beneath her fingers set up an answering beat in her own pulse.

"You once told me you had fallen in love, Bren," Fletch said quietly. "Tell me who with."

She had to swallow to relieve the constriction of her throat muscles. "You," she whispered, barely loud enough for him to hear.

"Me." He smiled softly, tenderly. Brushed a hand over her tumbling, hopelessly messy curls. "I fell in love a long, long time ago myself," Fletch said. "Never fell out of it, either. You?"

Bren couldn't speak. She shook her head slightly.

"But you knew you were in love," he murmured, his lips grazing across her brow. "I just knew all the women I met were, well, playmates but not life mates. I only just realized that I was in love with you. That I had been since the day you tried to jump Hobson's Creek and didn't make it."

His lips settled over the small half-moon scar on her temple, caressing it softly.

"It took your incessant pushing me toward marriage with Dominique to make me wise up," Fletch said. His lips feathered over her eyes, along her jawline. "But, you know, Bren, I've never wanted to spend my life with anyone but you. Not ever. Will you be my wife?"

He didn't let her answer, but slanted his mouth across hers, giving her a kiss that left Bren in no doubt that every word he'd said had been sincere. The way she was pressed to his body left her in no doubt that he wanted her as a woman as well as a friend.

"Fletch?" Bren murmured against his lips. She pushed back from the dizzying sensation of being in his arms and turned away, taking two steps into the room before swinging back to face him. "This is so unexpected."

He was as still as a statue. "And you know I'm no Prince Charming," he said, sounding defeated.

"No, you're not," Bren agreed, and she let her robe slip to the floor. "You're my knight errant, my protector, my hero. My best friend. I would love to be your wife, Fletch, but first..."

The daring courage that had once allowed her to swallow worms and attempt to leap her bike over Hobson's Creek now took her into new territory.

Bren shrugged the narrow straps of her nightgown off her shoulders. The silk slid to her waist and then lower, to join the pool of lace at her feet. "Could you be my lover?" she asked.

The trade show started without them that day. Much to Bren's delight, Fletch made it a point to prove the depth of his love for her quite thoroughly. They had one false start at going to work, but she'd barely got her pale stockings attached to the garters of her cream-colored teddy before he decided peeling her out of them was a far better idea. Bren had no complaints.

In fact, the melding of friendship and passion had been extraordinary. Better than even her wildest dreams. The best part was that when he gazed at her, Fletch's besotted expression was unlike any she'd ever seen him give another woman. He was truly hers now. As she was his. Always had been his.

"You know," Fletch mused when they finally made it into a taxi and were bound for the convention center. "I think we should get married here in Vegas before we go home."

"Here?" Bren stared at him as if he had sprouted antennae instead of cowlicks.

Just to be safe in either case, Fletch ran a hand over his hair, smoothing it into place. It was still damp from the shower, as was Bren's. She didn't seem to mind, and he thought she was even more delightful because of it.

"Hey," he insisted, "you more than anyone else know what a procrastinator I am. We can always have another ceremony at home for friends and family. Even share Josh and Sally's. But just in case we never get around to it, I'd like to make sure my children are relieved that I did manage to carry their mother to the altar."

"Children?" Bren repeated dreamily before getting back to the business at hand. "But I wouldn't feel right getting married without Mom and Dad and Josh and your parents there."

Fletch dropped a kiss on her lips. "I knew you'd feel that way," he said. "So I called them all last night and told them to get on the next flight available. They'll all be arriving tomorrow morning."

Bren's eyes grew wide. "You talked to them last night? Fletch! You hadn't even asked me yet. What if I'd said no?"

"Well, that's why I called them first, so I'd have backup arriving to convince you if need be," he said. "Believe me, I'm relieved you decided in my favor without any arm twisting."

Bren snuggled closer to him. "So am I. But we still have the trade show to wrap up tomorrow."

"Slave driver," he murmured. "Does this mean you're going to start nagging me?"

"I'll have to check what the book says about it," Bren said.

"Book?" he echoed.

She chewed on her bottom lip, looking mischievous. If they hadn't been pulling up to the main entrance of the convention center, Fletch would have been tempted to tell the driver to take them back to the hotel. To hell with work!

"Well, you see, Sally lent me this book she had," Bren confessed, her tone slightly apologetic as she fished in the large tote bag that had replaced the tiny purse she'd carried the day before. A moment later she handed over a thick volume.

"Land Your Man?" Fletch gasped in disbelief.

"Hey, don't laugh. It worked, didn't it?" Bren demanded.

He smiled, then chuckled, then burst into laughter. "Damn well, too."

"You don't mind, do you?" she asked.

"Mind?" Fletch said. "What do you think?"

The cabdriver had to clear his throat a couple times before either of them paid him any attention.

"It's about time you two showed up," Kurt grumbled when Fletch and Bren waltzed up to the Bailey and Salazar booth. "I can't find the rest of the samples we had yesterday."

Bren's hand flew to her lips. "Oops. I forgot to bring them. They're still back at the hotel. We'll have to open a new box. Fletch hustled me away from here too fast last night."

"So that's why I got stuck putting everything away on my own," Mick complained. "First Layton sends Kurt and Steve off with his bombshell—"

"Former bombshell," Fletch corrected. "I have a new bombshell now."

Steve clutched his chest dramatically. "Oh, God, no. It's not true!" he insisted, then dropped his head in his hands. "But she's glowing. Damn, it is true!"

Bren colored up even brighter.

"Behave yourselves and we'll invite you to the wedding tomorrow," Fletch said.

"W-w-wedding?" Mick stuttered. "Tomorrow? You're making an honest man of him, Bren?"

"Honest?" Fletch scoffed. "Please, don't insult me."

"Yeah," Steve added. "He is in sales, you know, not to mention the undisputed king of the B and S BSers."

Bren grinned happily. "He is, isn't he?"

"Which I shall now prove to everyone's satisfaction," Fletch said, and dazzled the very next visitor to stroll near their booth with a smile the equal of that on the Fresh All Day advertising posters.

"Do you want to know exactly how good this toothpaste is?" he asked the bemused customer, handing him a sample. "You see this lovely lady?"

Bren gave him a breathtaking grin as he drew her to his side.

"Well," Fletch confided, "I didn't even know she existed a week ago. But after she used Fresh All Day toothpaste for the full seven days, I had to give her an ultimatum. Marry me immediately or else."

Epilogue

◄►►◄

Day seven . . . and beyond

Fresh All Day smiles were in such evidence when the Laytons and Burtons gathered for Fletch and Bren's wedding that the justice of the peace was tempted to don sunglasses to cut the glare.

Fletch became a vice president, as expected. He beat his proclivity for procrastination so successfully that he not only was home for dinner on time every night, but he insisted upon choosing a name for their first child an hour after Bren told him she was pregnant.

Bren continued working in advertising, but turned down a promotion that would have taken her out of the creative arena and into management. She claimed, in declining, that managing Fletch was all she could handle.

Dominique recovered from Fletch's defection so quickly, no one was in doubt that her heart had been engaged, much less dented or broken. She actually beat Fletch and Bren to the altar by half an hour, eloping with a high roller she met at a blackjack table, and was last seen dragging her groom into a jewelry store.

And while her sister-in-law, Sally, continued to swear by the advice in *Land Your Man,* Bren wasn't surprised when she read that sales of the book were so feeble the publisher vowed never to issue another self-help guide of any kind. Looking back on events, Bren figured it hadn't been feminine ploys or well-thought-out strategies that had made her Fletch's wife. It had been love. Wonderful, glorious love.

*   *   *   *   *

*'Tis the season for
holiday weddings!*

This December, celebrate the holidays
with two sparkling new love stories—
only from

 VSILHOUETTE YOURS TRULY™

A Nice Girl Like You
by Alexandra Sellers

Sara Diamond may be a nice girl, but that doesn't mean
she wants to be Ben Harris's ideal bride. But she might
just be able to play Ms. Wrong long enough to help this
confirmed bachelor find his true wife! That is, if she
doesn't fall in love first....

 ## A Marry-Me Christmas
by Jo Ann Algermissen

All Catherine Jordan wanted for Christmas was some
time away from the hustle and bustle. Now she was
sharing a wilderness cabin with her infuriating opposite,
Stone Scofield! But once she stood under the mistletoe
with Stone, she was hoping for a whole lot more
this holiday....

 Don't miss these exciting new books,
our gift to you this holiday season!

Look us up on-line at: http://www.romance.net

XMASYT

Concluding in November from Silhouette books...

This exciting new cross-line continuity series unites five
of your favorite authors as they weave five connected
novels about love, marriage—and Daddy's unexpected
need for a baby carriage!

You fell in love with the wonderful characters in:

THE BABY NOTION by Dixie Browning (Desire 7/96)

BABY IN A BASKET by Helen R. Myers
(Romance 8/96)

MARRIED...WITH TWINS! by Jennifer Mikels
(Special Edition 9/96)

HOW TO HOOK A HUSBAND (AND A BABY)
by Carolyn Zane (Yours Truly 10/96)

And now all of your questions will finally be answered in

DISCOVERED: DADDY
by Marilyn Pappano (Intimate Moments 11/96)

Everybody is still wondering...who's the father of prim and
proper Faith Harper's baby? But Faith isn't letting anyone
in on her secret—not until she informs the daddy-to-be.
Trouble is, *he* doesn't seem to remember her....

Don't miss the exciting conclusion of
DADDY KNOWS LAST...only in Silhouette books!

FORTUNE'S Children™

Bestselling Author
LINDA TURNER

Continues the twelve-book series—FORTUNE'S CHILDREN—
in November 1996 with Book Five

THE WOLF AND THE DOVE

Adventurous pilot Rachel Fortune and traditional Native American
doctor Luke Greywolf set sparks off each other the minute they met.
But widower Luke was tormented by guilt and vowed never to love
again. Could tempting Rachel heal Luke's wounded heart so they
could share a future of happily ever after?

MEET THE FORTUNES—a family whose legacy is greater than riches.
Because where there's a will…there's a *wedding!*

A CASTING CALL TO
ALL FORTUNE'S CHILDREN FANS!
If you are truly fortunate,
you may win a trip to
Los Angeles to audition for
Wheel of Fortune®. Look for
details in all retail Fortune's Children titles!

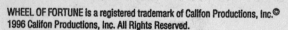

Look us up on-line at: http://www.romance.net

FC-5-C

The collection of the year!
NEW YORK TIMES BESTSELLING AUTHORS

Linda Lael Miller
Wild About Harry

Janet Dailey
Sweet Promise

Elizabeth Lowell
Reckless Love

Penny Jordan
Love's Choices

and featuring
Nora Roberts
The Calhoun Women

This special trade-size edition features four of the wildly popular titles in the Calhoun miniseries together in one volume—a true collector's item!

Pick up these great authors and a chance to win a weekend for two in New York City at the Marriott Marquis Hotel on Broadway! We'll pay for your flight, your hotel—even a Broadway show!

Available in December at your favorite retail outlet.

NEW YORK
Marriott®
MARQUIS

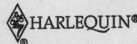 

1997
Reader's Engagement Book
A calendar of important dates
and anniversaries for readers to use!

Informative and entertaining—with notable
dates and trivia highlighted throughout the year.

Handy, convenient, pocketbook size to help you
keep track of your own personal important dates.

Added bonus—contains $5.00 worth of coupons
for upcoming Harlequin and Silhouette books.
This calendar more than pays for itself!

Available beginning in November at
your favorite retail outlet.